Danny Dingle's Fantastic Finds

Sweet Cherry
Publishing

Published by Sweet Cherry Publishing Limited
Unit E, Vulcan Business Complex
Vulcan Road
Leicester, LE5 3EB
United Kingdom

www.sweetcherrypublishing.com

First published in the UK in 2015
ISBN: 978-1-78226-208-4

Illustrated by Suruchi Sati and Shanith MM

Danny Dingle's Fantastic Finds: The Metal-Mobile

Printed and bound by Thomson Press (India) Limited.

Danny Dingle's Fantastic Finds

Book 1

The Metal-Mobile

DANNY DINGLE'S SUPER-SECRET SPY NOTEBOOK.

DO NOT READ (unless you are Danny, Percy or Superdog.)

Just don't.

Seriously, **DON'T.**

I'm not joking!

BE WARNED: if you turn the page, this notebook will **EXPLODE!**

BOOM

TOLD YA!

Anyway,

This is me, Danny Dingle.

Although I'm still at school at the moment, I will one day be an inventor and will spend ALL DAY making cool contraptions for

THE WORLD'S BEST SUPERHERO:

METAL FACE

Metal Face is the absolute **BEST** superhero in the world.

Why?

Well, because of his secret weapon, of course!

His secret weapon?

GAS, what else?

His burps are **SO LOUD** that he can

BLOW OUT

YOUR EARDRUMS

His supersonic farts are SO **POWERFUL** that he can strip the paint off a door!

(If he sits on the floor and farts, he can start a

FARTQUAKE!)

Percy (my assistant) and I studied this phenomenon last week at school.

We prepared by each eating A WHOLE TIN OF...

BAKED
BEANS

No, we didn't start any FARTQUAKES.

But we DID find that the marble floor in the science room was the best (and funniest) surface for the transmission of a loud fart.

That is until Mr Hammond, the science teacher, busted us!

He wanted to know what we were doing sitting on the floor with our trousers down.

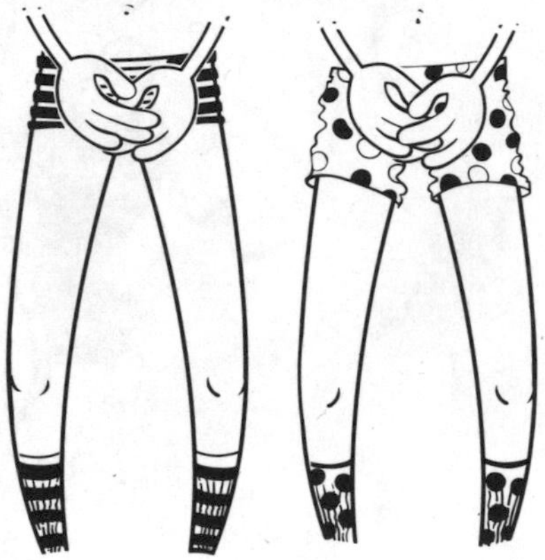

I said that we were conducting an experiment to find out how VIBRATIONS travel through different surfaces.

He didn't believe me, 

but he said that my explanation was "very clever" (I **AM** a bit of a genius).

KNOCK IT OFF BOYS!

These were his exact words.

This is a picture of Percy McDuff, my assistant.

He helps me with my experiments and sits next to me in class.

Although I like sitting next to Percy, I sometimes wish I could sit next to someone who doesn't fail at **EVERYTHING.**

It would be nice to have someone smart to copy from for a change.

Percy says that it's my fault that he fails everything because **HE COPIES HIS WORK FROM ME!**

Typical. 

F

At the moment I live in Greenville in a house with my mum, dad and baby sister, Mel.

This is all just a bit too normal and **BORING** for me.

When I grow up and go to work for Metal Face, I will live somewhere COOL!

Like inside a volcano!

...Or under the sea!

...Or on a satellite orbiting a nearby planet!

You see, the most important thing about being an inventor is knowing how to use normal everyday stuff (boring) to make other MUCH COOLER STUFF (COOL!).

For example:

NORMAL
COOLER

For this reason I take my...

SPECIAL INVENTOR'S KIT

with me EVERYWHERE so I can collect any cool stuff I find lying about.

RULES FOR INVENTORS #1:

You must **ALWAYS** be on the lookout for...

COOL STUFF

EXAMPLES OF
COOL
STUFF
YOU MIGHT FIND
springs
pen caps
yogurt cup
shoe lace
A handkerchief
Roller skates

What can you make with all that, I hear you ask?

Erm, let's see . . .

Ooh, maybe something like....

THIS
TADA

A SPECIAL SPY VEHICLE WITH AN EMERGENCY EJECTOR SEAT!

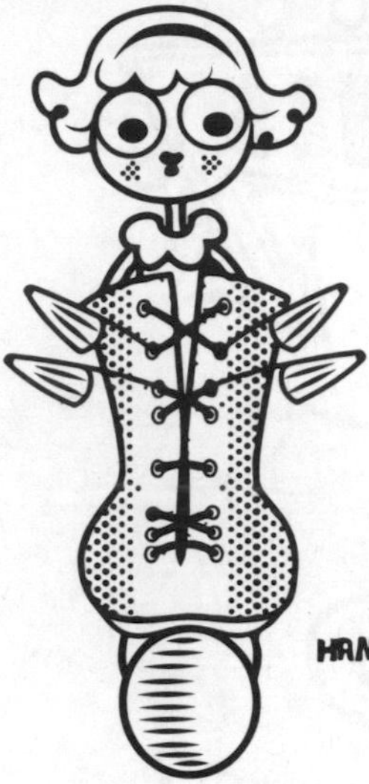

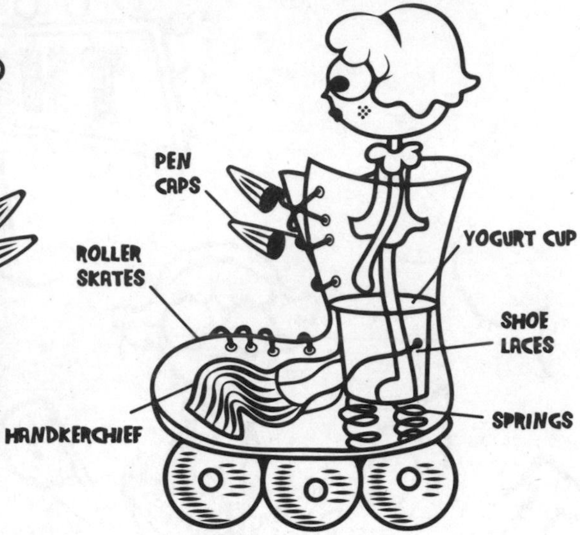
PEN CAPS
YOGURT CUP
ROLLER SKATES
SHOE LACES
SPRINGS
HANDKERCHIEF

##!!
!

AAAAaaaaaa

SUCCESS

In order for you to collect all the COOL STUFF that you might find lying around, you'll need to carry a **SPECIAL INVENTOR'S KIT** too!

My super-secret, super-special inventor's kit contains:

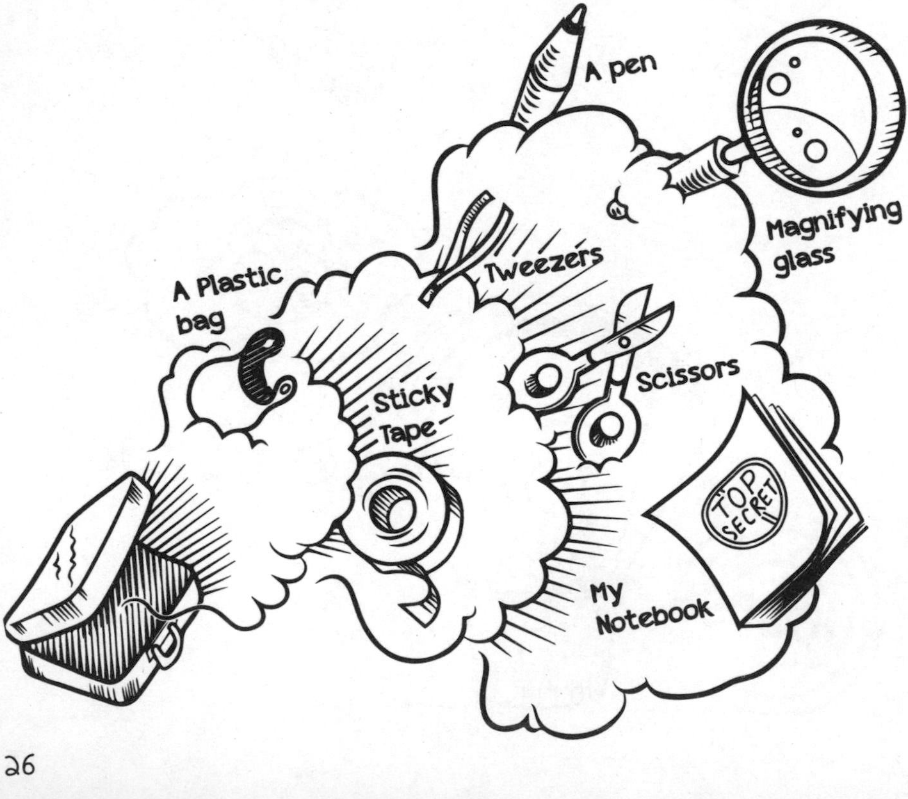
A pen
Magnifying glass
Tweezers
A Plastic bag
Scissors
Sticky Tape
TOP SECRET
My Notebook

This morning on my way to school I found this REALLY cool stuff:

A chewed-up chewing gum
&
A box of Rubberbands
RUBBERBANDS

Mum doesn't let me pick up chewed-up pieces of chewing gum because she thinks that it's "DISGUSTING!"

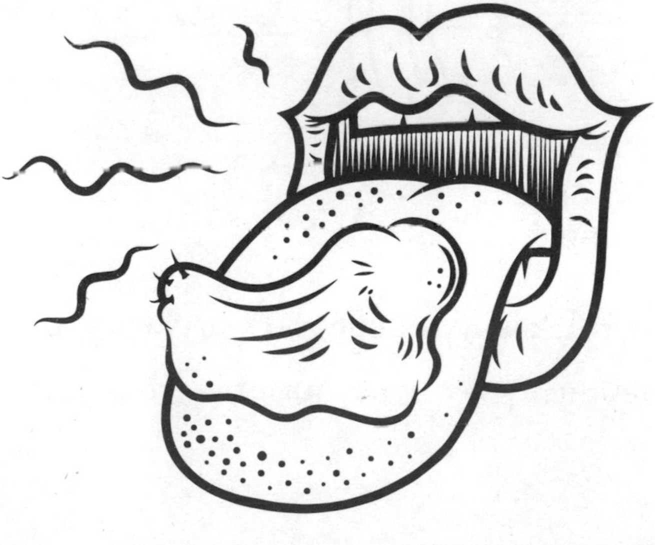

Even Percy says that it makes him "want to BARF!"

But I always collect it anyway when no one is looking because, let's be honest, it's just so USEFUL!

After school, Percy and I went to our secret laboratory.

In order to remain a secret, our secret laboratory has been cleverly (and secretly) disguised as a clubhouse.

NORMAL CLUBHOUSE
KEEP OUT

Which is very clever, even if I do say so myself (and I do – in secret).

Percy catalogued my **FANTASTIC FINDS** in the jam jars and shoeboxes we keep for this super all-important purpose.

Then Percy and I ate some of the baked bean jelly that Dad had brought round (yes, **BAKED BEAN JELLY** - all will be revealed . . .) and got on with some inventing.

No one knows the secret truth about our secret laboratory: only Percy, Superdog and my dad.

ELITE MEMBERS OF
Me
Percy
Dad
?
Superdog
THE SECRET LAB

This is SUPERDOG.

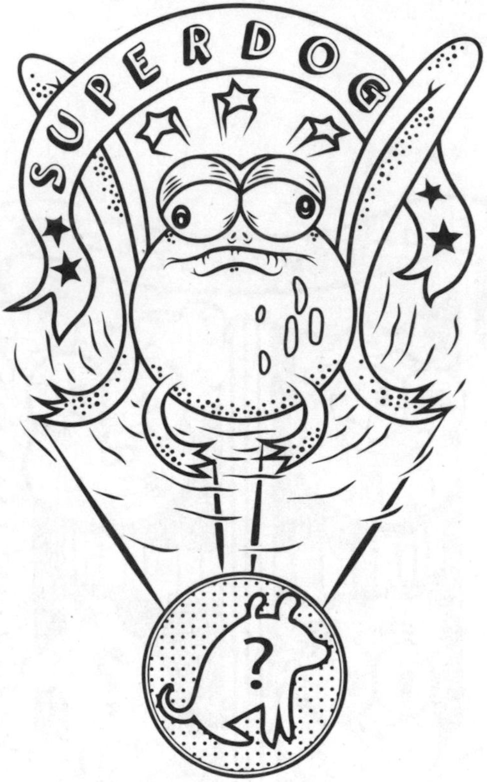
SUPERDOG
?

As you can see, Superdog isn't exactly a dog.

He is, technically speaking, more of a toad.

You may be asking yourself:

1) Why would anyone have a pet toad?

2) Why would anyone call their pet toad Superdog?

It's a bit of a long story, so brace yourselves:

For years I've wanted a dog, but Mum and Dad have never been particularly keen on the idea:

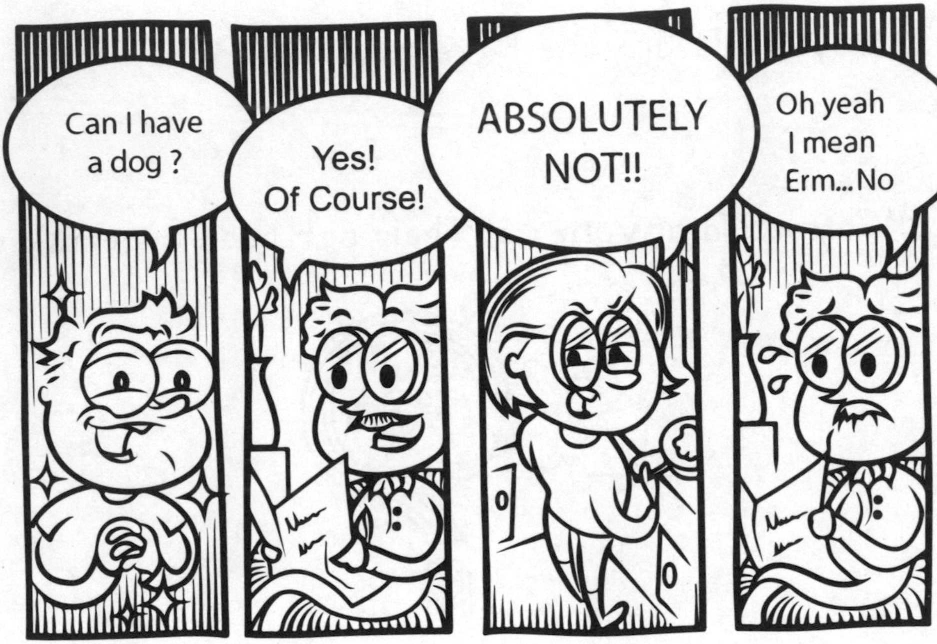
Can I have a dog ?
Yes! Of Course!
ABSOLUTELY NOT!!
Oh yeah I mean Erm... No

I tried all sorts of methods to get them to change their minds, using negotiation techniques crafted by generations of crafty technical negotiators.

These included:

- **BRIBERY:**

Me: Can I get a dog if I get an A in Art?

Mum: No, but you can get a dog if you get an A in Maths.

D-

- REPETITION:

Me: Can I get a dog? Can I? Can I? Can I? Can I? PLEASE? PLEASE? PLEASE? PLEASE? PLEASE? (You get the idea.)

PLEASE
PLEASE

Mum: No.

- . . . SONG?

I really wish I had a dog
To take out walking in the fog...
I'd feed and walk him every day
And with the dog I'd always play...

I really wish I had a dog
To take out walking in the fog...
And if he pooed upon the floor
I'd throw it out the kitchen door...

sing that song one more time...
...and you can get out and walk home.

Finally I had a GENIUS IDEA

I created a...

DOG TRAP

All I needed was:

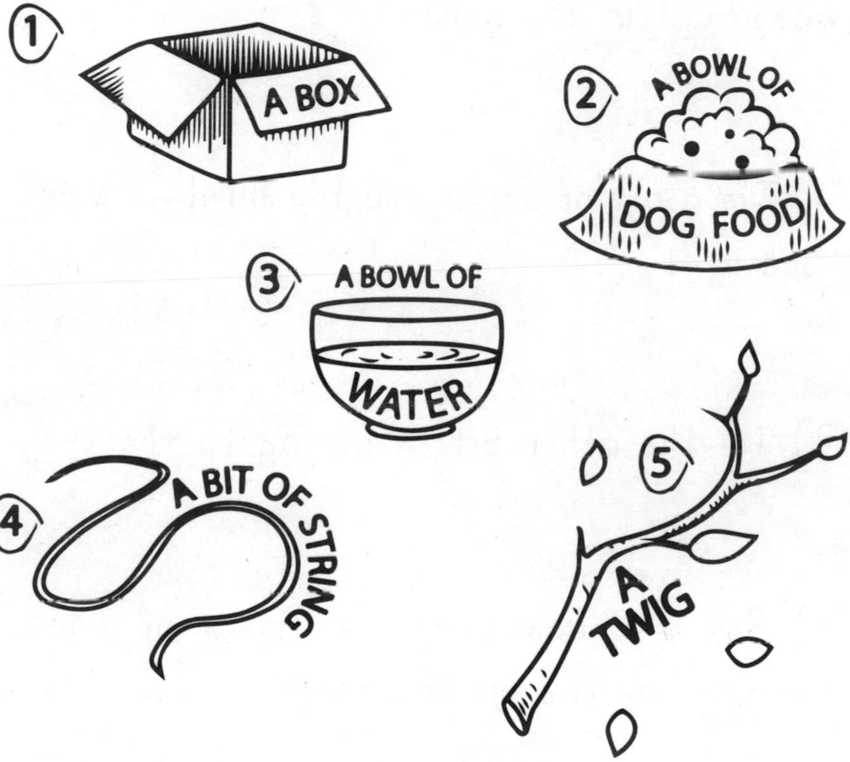

1
A BOX
2
A BOWL OF
DOG FOOD
3
A BOWL OF
WATER
4
A BIT OF STRING
5
A TWIG

How to Work a **Dog Trap**:

1) Put the bowl of dog food and the bowl of water out in the garden

2) Tie a bit of string to the bowl with the dog food in it

3) Tie the other bit of string to the twig

4) Put the box over the bowls of food and balance one end on the twig

In theory, when a dog ate the food it would move the bowl.

The bowl is tied to the string and that string would pull the twig.

The twig would be pulled out from under the box, and the box would fall over the dog.

SUCCESS!

SUCCESS

In theory.

Looking back on it now, I realise that if I had wanted to catch a dog-sized dog I would probably have needed something bigger than a shoebox . . .

Anyway,

I set the trap on a warm Friday evening, and in the morning I found that I had captured . . .

SUPERDOG!

I took Superdog indoors to ask Mum and Dad if I could keep him.

When Dad saw Superdog he thought he was, and I quote, "BRILLIANT!"

When Mum saw Superdog, she was less enthusiastic:

BRILLIANT!!!
Oh, for goodness sake...

Superdog is actually 
Genius
, but he's in disguise.

He has also mastered the powers of hypnosis and telepathy.

Well, he can read **MY** mind.

I can't read his because I'm not a **PSYCHIC TOAD**.

Despite his abilities, Superdog is (like ALL geniuses – me included) misunderstood and not allowed in the house (luckily, I AM allowed in the house).

This is largely because of:

- The time he had a bath with Mum

- The time Mum found him playing with Mel

SLURP!

- The time Mum found him watching the match with Dad

And he's **DEFINITELY** not allowed in school.

This is probably because of the time he was spotted by Miss Quimby and she fainted.

Ms.

Fortunately she was rescued by our headmaster, Mr Norton, who cleverly wafted a doughnut under her nose (she loves doughnuts).

Mmmmm...doughnuts.....

Everyone else in school thought that Superdog was **WICKED!**

That includes:

- My best friend and assistant Percy McDuff

- Debra Kirby from the Roller Derby, who is really very nice but FREAKISHLY STRONG for a girl

- Debra Kirby's friend, Amy Almond, who wants to grow up to be a welder

Even Mr Hammond thought that Superdog was "very interesting".

Hmmm.... Interesting!

As did Ms Mills, the PE teacher:

Danny Dingle, you get that thing out of my face !!

Ms Mills used to be in the Army.

She doesn't usually suffer fools gladly (although she'll gladly make fools suffer), so I considered this quite a compliment coming from her.

Ms Mills fancies Mr Hammond.

It's **OBVIOUS!**

He is also OBVIOUSLY quite scared of her (who isn't?) and often hides when she's nearby.

Mr Norton (the headmaster) didn't really seem to care about Superdog.

He doesn't really seem to care about much at all.

What he **DOES** care about, however, is his hair – or, that is, the lack of it.

So Superdog has to live in my ~~laboratory~~ CLUBHOUSE.

My clubhouse is at the end of my garden, and Percy often comes over to help me with my inventions.

Dad is also an inventor, but his specialty is making potions and concoctions.

At the moment we are testing the...

POWER OF GAS

This is **VERY IMPORTANT** research for Percy and me.

Dad has been very helpful.

Last Saturday, he spent all day in the kitchen helping us develop **THE MOST POTENT GAS POTION IN THE WORLD** to help Metal Face enhance his superpowers (Mum had gone out).

He made:

- Baked bean and sprout jelly

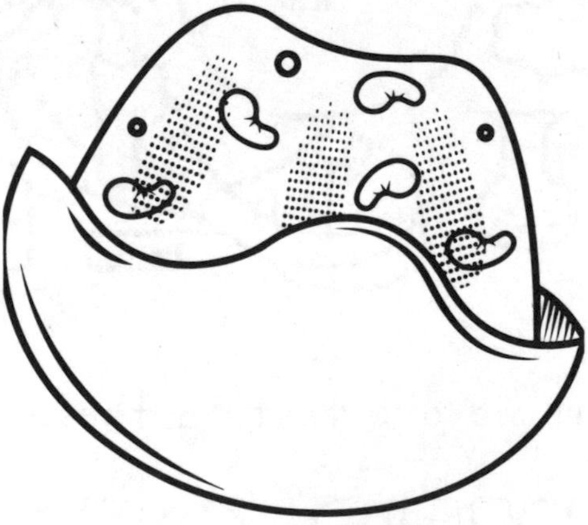

AND

- Cabbage, sprout and chickpea mash

Needless to say, the house stank ALL WEEKEND!

We were all very pleased.

Dad IS a genius though.

Now he's working on a super-secret recipe for

SUPER-FIZZY SPROUT COLA!

SC
Sprout
Cola

Percy and I have also been very busy.

We've been working on a SPECTACULAR NEW INVENTION over the past few weeks:

A SUPER-SECRET SPY SATELLITE!

SUPER SECRET
SPY SATELLITE

This is what we have used to build it:

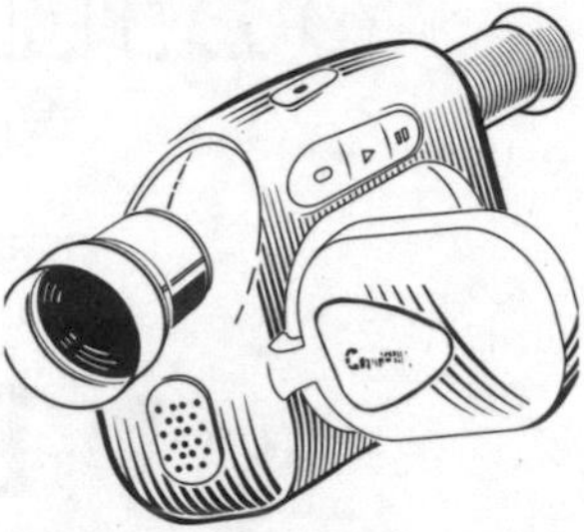

- Mum's video camera

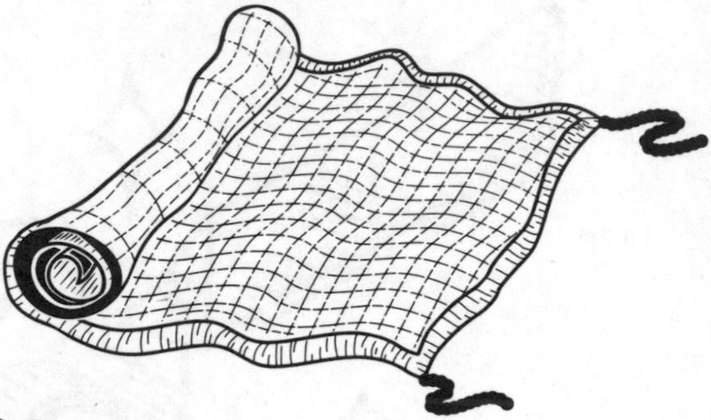

- A badminton net

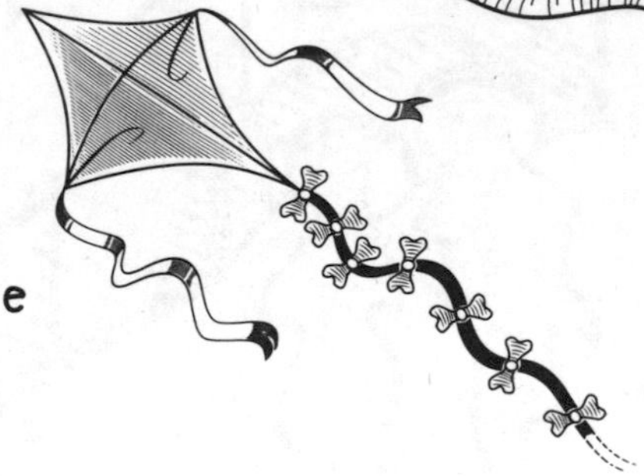

- A kite

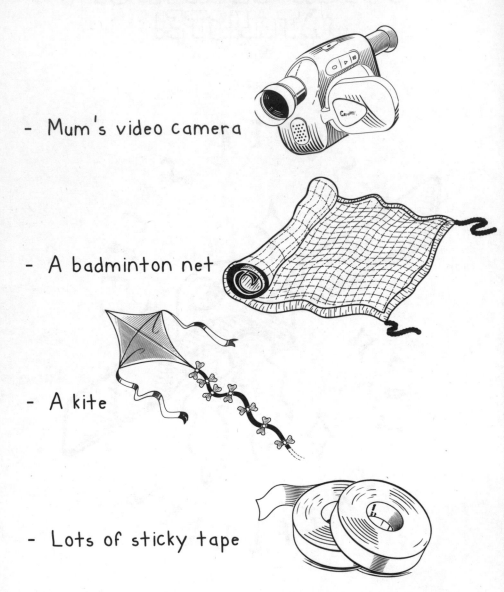

- Lots of sticky tape

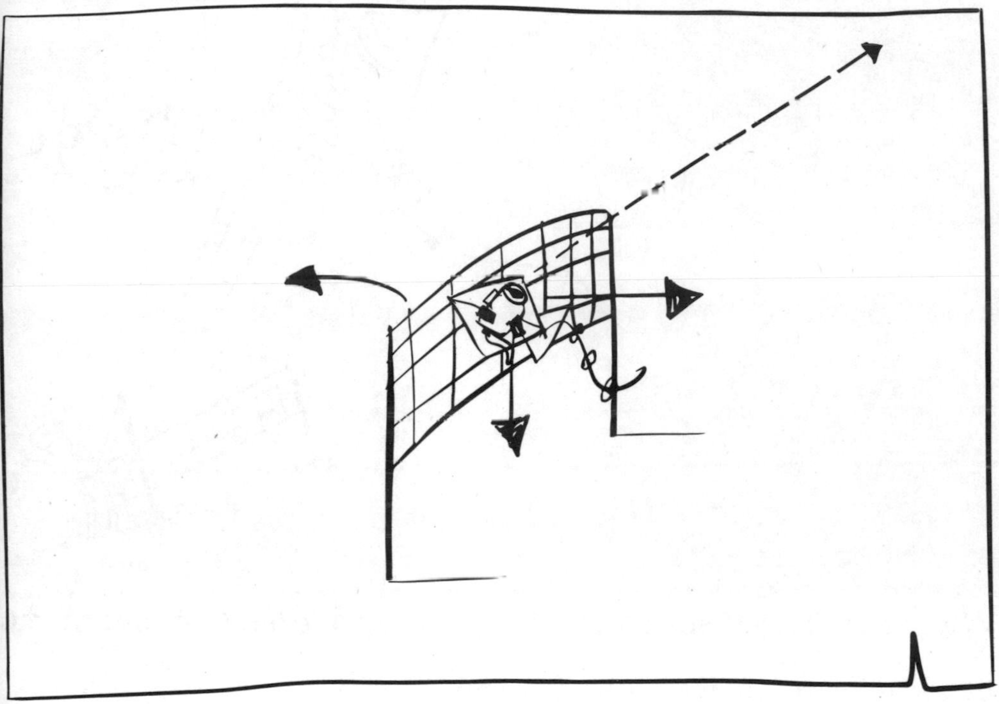

The launch tests have been quite successful so far, but we're having a TINY WEENIE bit of trouble getting it to stay in orbit.

We have noticed that the camera doesn't seem to be working as well as it used to.

We suspect that this is because it has been quite smashed up.

But I'm sure that we will be able to fix this problem (and certain other minor issues) once we have manage to get the satellite to actually STAY IN ORBIT!

We HAD considered getting Superdog to pilot the satellite, but he wasn't the most willing of astronauts.

NOT A CHANCE

Today I woke up feeling EXCITED!

Percy was going to come over after school so we could do more work on the spy satellite!

AND Dad said there was still some baked bean jelly left over!

AND he had a special surprise to help us with our spy satellite.

EXCITING!

Mum said that Percy could stay for tea and left Dad instructions to clean the house.

I agreed that Percy should stay for tea and left Superdog instructions to fix the camera.

Unfortunately, I still had to get through a WHOLE DAY at school.

I just about managed to sit though English without falling asleep, but the day was dragging on and it was only going to get worse because the next lesson was MATHS (BLEURGH!).

For some dreadful reason, time seems to FREEZE in Maths class (BLEURGH!).

+
2
-
6
4
1

Today, we had to draw a grid with positive numbers and negative numbers on it and mark different coordinates.

I decided that the easiest way to solve this problem was to draw a real person on the grid that could walk to the different coordinates all by themselves, which would save me from having to figure it out (I AM a genius, after all).

I picked up my pencil . . . but who could I draw that would be up to the task?

BINGO!

I decided to draw Ms Mills.

The only problem is that she's SO

BIG & SCARY

that she took up the whole grid!

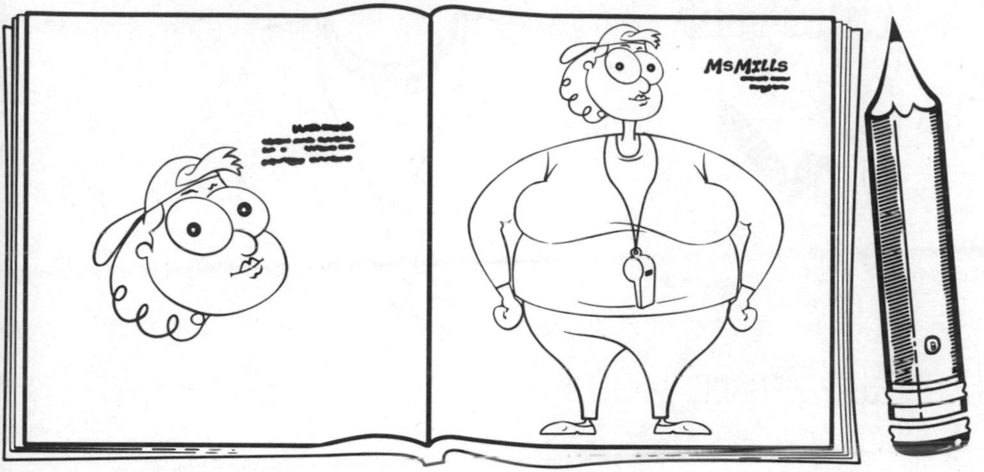
MsMills

I tried to get all the details right:

- **FACE LIKE A BULLDOG?**

Check ✔

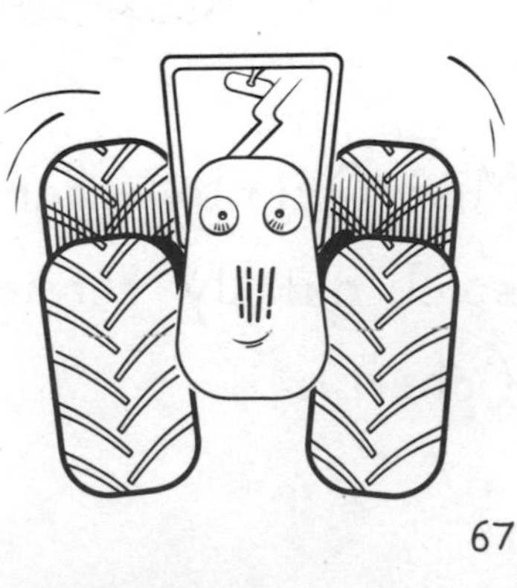

- **BODY LIKE A TRACTOR?**

Check ✔

- **WHISTLE?**

Check ✓

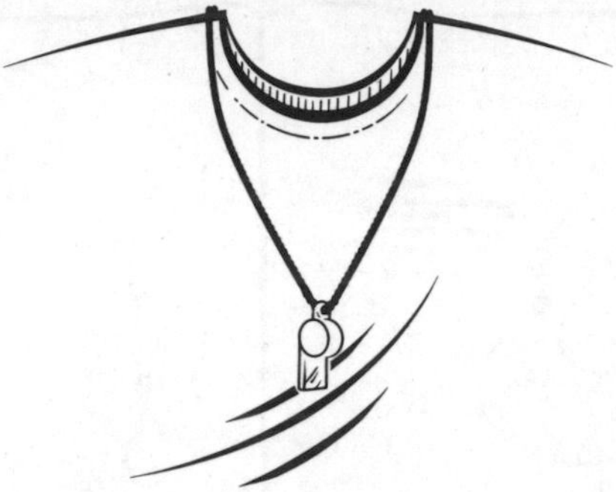

- **RED FACE . . .**

UH-OH!

Miss Quimby started walking towads me (ARGH!), so I quickly turned my page to some old homework (phew).

Miss Quimby came over and said to me:

I THOUGHT ID COME OVER AND HAVE A LOOK AT WHAT YOU WERE UP TO: LAST WEEKS HOMEWORK, IT SEEMS.DONT WORRY THOUGH; YOUR FRIEND PERCY HERE HAS BEEN COPYING YOU ALL MORNING. LET'S SEE WHAT HES DONE...

OH NO!

Percy had copied my picture too!

Why, Percy, WHY?

Miss Quimby looked carefully at the picture and said:

BOYS, THIS IS NOT THE WORK I ASKED YOU TO DO...BUT (SHE SNIGGERS AT PERCY'S MS. MILLS) I'M GOING TO ALLOW THIS - THIS ONCE.

So Percy and I spent the rest of Maths putting the finishing touches to our drawings of Ms Mills.

RESULT!

At break time, Percy and I saw Debra Derby and Amy Almond.

They were eating packets of **JELLY SQUARES!**

Jelly is the best food EVER!

You can put something in it and it will get stuck as though it's been hit by a freeze ray!

Metal Face eats lots of jelly (I think that this is where he gets his strength from).

This makes perfect sense because Debra Derby is freakishly strong AND eats jelly squares.

FLEXING MUSCLES

This reminded me that Percy and I had my Dad's baked bean jelly to look forward to when we get home.

We have agreed that it tastes absolutely GROSS but that it does give us wicked **FART-POWER!**

When Percy and I finally got to my secret laboratory (sorry, CLUBHOUSE) we found that Superdog hadn't been working on the spy satellite at all.

(That is okay though, because Superdog is a GENIUS and needs lots of creative freedom.)

Instead, Superdog had taken a mud bath and eaten a beetle.

Percy said that he was going to barf (as usual).

I told Percy that he's a lightweight (as usual).

Dad soon came to the rescue with his baked bean jelly and his surprise.

As it turned out, Dad's surprise was something that he had "borrowed" from Mum.

It was . . .

A FITNESS TRAMPOLINE

Dad suggested that we should use it to put the satellite into orbit.

This was a GENIUS idea (told you he was a genius).

We tried bouncing the satellite off the trampoline, but it didn't really go very far.

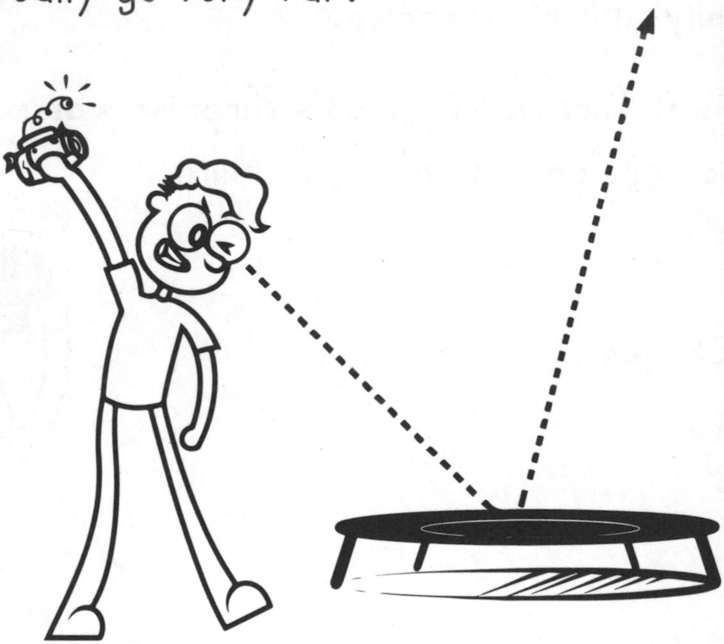

Then Dad suggested that **WE** bounce on the trampoline, and then, once we'd bounced as high as we could, we should throw the satellite up into orbit.

We all took turns at this, but we didn't have much luck.

The satellite looked a LITTLE worse for wear (bits of it kept flying off).

Eventually, Dad had an idea.

The BEST idea of all.

As the tallest, Dad decided that HE should jump up and down on the trampoline.

Then, when he was bouncing REALLY high, we should throw the satellite up to him so that he could WHACK it into orbit with his trusty cricket bat.

It went up quite far . . . but it didn't stay up for long.

Also, a lot more bits flew off.

Also, Dad put his foot though the trampoline and broke it.

We decided to call it a day.

Before tea, Dad suggested that we should put everything neatly away (throw it in the bin) and clean up the "crime scene" (I think he meant the "garden") before Mum got home.

Whilst Mum and Dad made tea, Percy and I sat in the living room watching TV, seeing who could do the loudest fart:

HERE COMES A BIG ONE!
I CAN MAKE MINE LAST LONGER!
NRR..!!
NRR...!!!

Knock it off boys, this isn't a farmyard!

Then something flashed up on the TV.

Something BRILLIANT!

Something AMAZING!

Something FANTASTIC!

It turned out that . . .

(Wait for it . . .)

THE NEW METAL FACE MOVIE WAS ABOUT TO COME OUT!!!

METAL FACE
THE MOVIE
HURRAY HURRAY!!

HURRAY FOR EVERYTHING!

Over tea (which I didn't really fancy, seeing as I was already so FULL OF GAS) I decided to discuss the possibility of going to see the movie with Mum and Dad:

CAN I GO TO SEE THE NEW METAL FACE MOVIE ?
NO WAY JOSE.
I'LL GO WITH YOU.
OH YEAH -ERM, I MEAN... WE'LL HAVE TO DISCUSS IT

So I tried a different tactic:

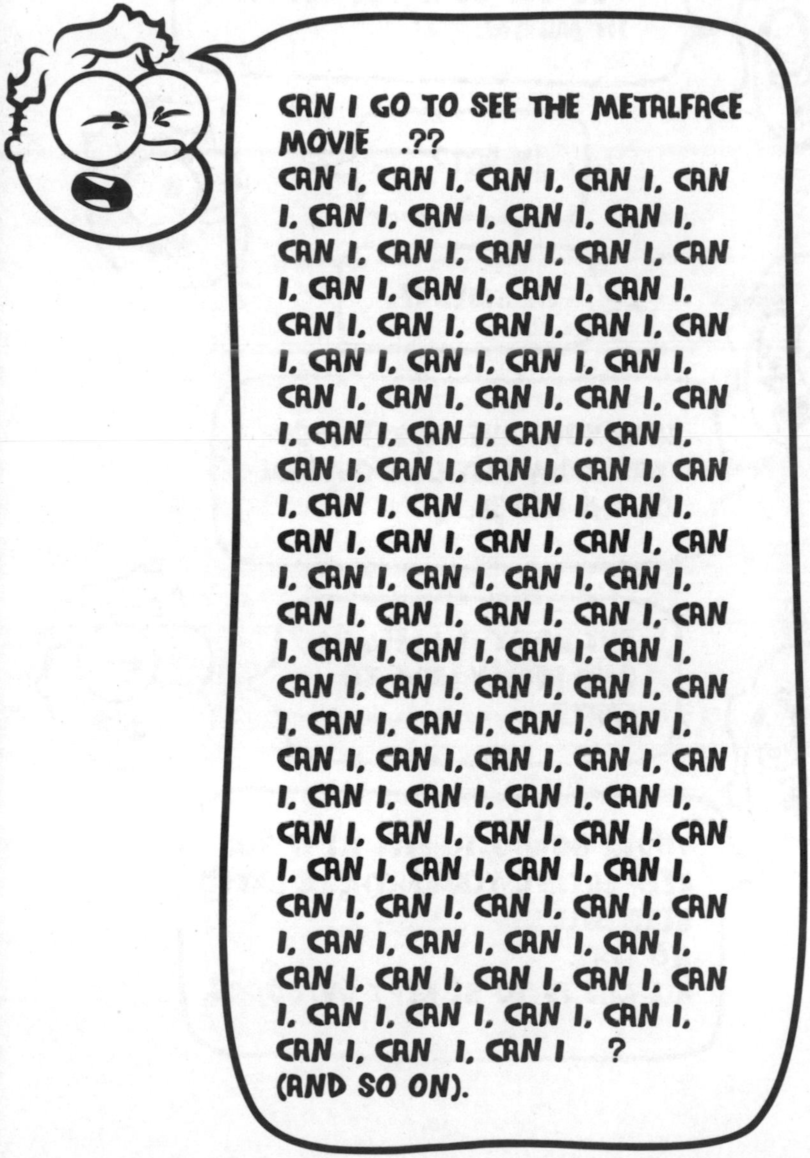
CAN I GO TO SEE THE METALFACE
MOVIE .??
CAN I, CAN I, CAN I, CAN I, CAN
I, CAN I, CAN I, CAN I, CAN I,
CAN I, CAN I, CAN I, CAN I, CAN
I, CAN I, CAN I, CAN I, CAN I,
CAN I, CAN I, CAN I, CAN I, CAN
I, CAN I, CAN I, CAN I, CAN I,
CAN I, CAN I, CAN I, CAN I, CAN
I, CAN I, CAN I, CAN I, CAN I,
CAN I, CAN I, CAN I, CAN I, CAN
I, CAN I, CAN I, CAN I, CAN I,
CAN I, CAN I, CAN I, CAN I, CAN
I, CAN I, CAN I, CAN I, CAN I,
CAN I, CAN I, CAN I, CAN I, CAN
I, CAN I, CAN I, CAN I, CAN I,
CAN I, CAN I, CAN I, CAN I, CAN
I, CAN I, CAN I, CAN I, CAN I,
CAN I, CAN I, CAN I, CAN I, CAN
I, CAN I, CAN I, CAN I, CAN I,
CAN I, CAN I, CAN I, CAN I, CAN
I, CAN I, CAN I, CAN I, CAN I,
CAN I, CAN I, CAN I, CAN I, CAN
I, CAN I, CAN I, CAN I, CAN I,
CAN I, CAN I, CAN I, CAN I, CAN
I, CAN I, CAN I, CAN I, CAN I,
CAN I, CAN I, CAN I ?
(AND SO ON).

YOU CAN GO IF YOU GET AN A IN MATHS.
IN ART?
IN SCIENCE.
AND YOU HAVE TO KEEP YOUR 'GAS' COMPETITIONS OUTSIDE OF THE HOUSE.
BUT WHAT IF I FEEL ILL AND REALLY HAVE TO FART?
YOU'RE BOUND TO FEEL ILL IF YOU KEEP EATING YOUR FATHER'S BAKED BEAN JELLY.
NO WAY.
ALL GAS IS TO BE KEPT OUTDOORS.

After tea, Percy and I went back out into the garden to release some gas and feed Superdog.

We discussed the new **METAL FACE** movie.

Apparently there was this new villain in town. His name was. . .

PUDDING BREATH

Pudding Breath is Metal Face's ~~nemen nema nemi~~ enemy.

Pudding Breath has the power to COUGH UP CURDLED CUSTARD!

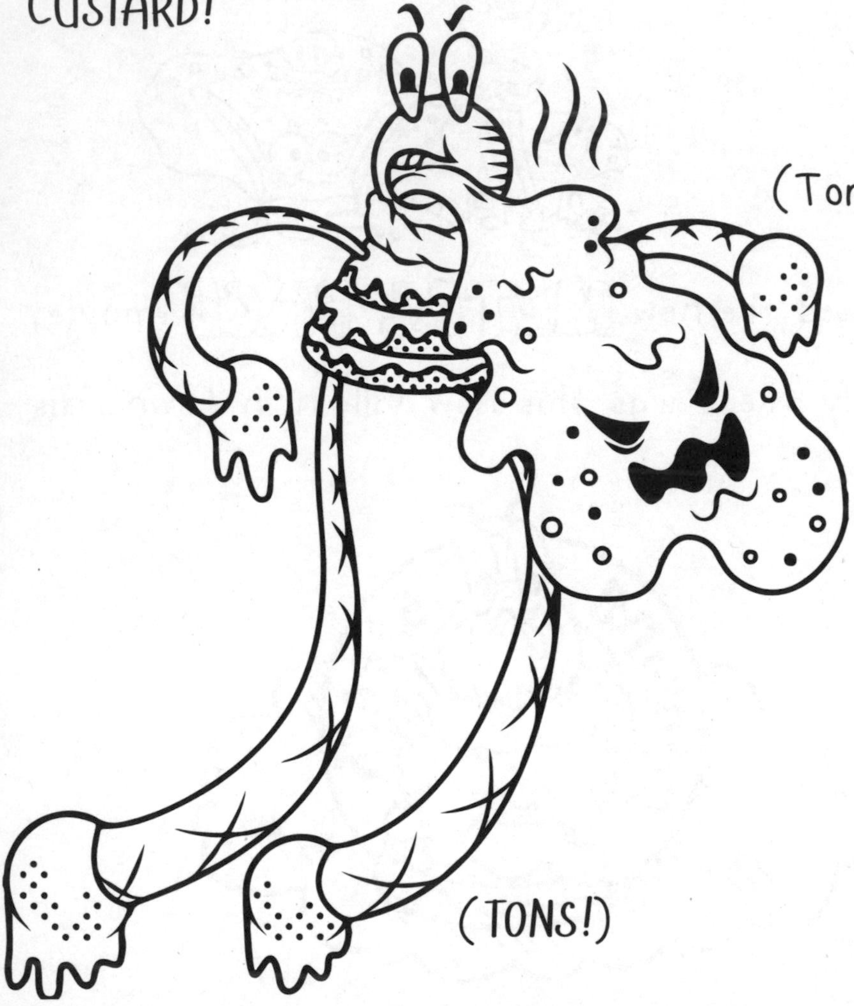
(Tons of it.)
(TONS!)

I didn't mention it to Percy at the time but I was secretly a bit worried that he might be tempted to go and work for Pudding Breath one day, seeing as he also had the ability to puke up on command.

Well, not exactly "on command" . . .

At will.

Well, not exactly "at will" . . .

Basically, he pukes quite a lot.

Percy has been known to barf because:

- I've handed him a ball of "recycled" chewing gum

- He's seen a dead mouse

- Superdog has eaten a beetle in front of him

- Superdog has thrown up after eating a beetle in front of him

Once we'd finished poisoning the plant life in the garden, we went inside.

I went into the kitchen and started rummaging through the cupboards.

Mum wanted to know what I was looking for.

I'M JUST LOOKING TO SEE IF WE HAVE ANY CUSTARD POWDER.
WE HAVEN'T GOT ANY

Phew!

We don't want Percy getting any ideas . . .

SCHOOL...

On my way to school today I found the following...

Cool Stuff
A BENT PAPERCLIP
50
FIFTY PENCE
A BROKEN BELT
A FIFTY PENCE COIN

RESULT!

When I got to school I gave Percy the belt and the paperclip to catalogue, but I decided to keep the coin safe (in my pocket).

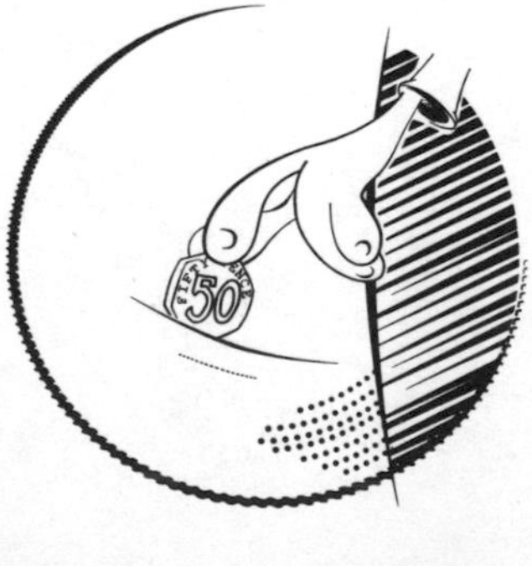

The morning was off to a GREAT start.

Then Miss Quimby came in looking REALLY GRUMPY.

None of us said anything because we all knew better, but it was clear that she hasn't had her usual morning doughnut.

(And we all know that you dough-nut cross someone when they're hungry!)(Hahaha!)

I told Percy that we would have to give her a **w i d e** berth today.

Percy asked me what I meant.

I had to think about this for a bit.

I wasn't sure, but my granddad says it all the time and I was pretty sure that it has something to do with ships.

Percy said that Miss Quimby has a bum "as WIDE as a ship" and that you'd need "a VERY WIDE space to sail around it".

Hahaha! 

Percy and I giggled and Miss Quimby told us to be quiet:

YOU TWO!!
KNOCK IT OFF.

I spent the rest of the morning doodling an island in the middle of the sea.

It was a big island, and looked SURPRISINGLY like Miss Quimby's bum . . .

MISS QUIMBY'S BUM.

Percy saw my HILARIOUS doodle.

He added a lighthouse.

I added some seagulls.

PERCY ADDS A LIGHTHOUSE
I ADD SOME SEAGULLS FLYING

Percy and I spent the morning adding more COOL STUFF to Bum Cheek Island.

Before we knew it, it was time for Science Club, which is our

ABSOLUTE ALL-TIME FAVORITE (school) ACTIVITY

Although it's not as good as inventing stuff in my secret laboratory (I mean, CLUBHOUSE) because

- Superdog isn't allowed to come and help

- We're not allowed to eat jelly and/or fart

- We don't get to borrow things from my mum

We have to put up with smug, full-of-himself, twit-faced Gareth Trumpshaw

GARETH
1ST PRIZE

He's a complete IDIOT.

He thinks that all of his inventions are the best but it's not fair because he cheats on ALL the challenges!

Smug, full-of-himself, twit-faced Gareth's dad works at AcmeTech.

He develops technology for

TOP-SECRET IMPORTANT STUFF like:

- DRINKS DISPENSING MACHINES

HERE'S YOUR COFFEE! WHITE, ONE SUGAR.

- SANDWICH DISPENSING MACHINES

HERE'S YOUR SANDWICH: CHEESE AND PICKLE.

- AND... ERM... CAT DISPENSING MACHINES?

HERE'S YOUR CAT: BLACK KITTEN, GREEN EYES.
THEY'RE ALWAYS OUT OF TABBY'S BY THIS TIME OF THE DAY.

(Actually, I'm not sure about that last one – sounds a bit made-up.)

So I was busy thinking about all the different types of dispensing machines that you could have:

- **PEN DISPENSING MACHINES**

- **PHONE DISPENSING MACHINES**

- TOOTHPASTE DISPENSING MACHINES

- EGG DISPENSING MACHINES

Yeah, maybe not eggs.

Anyway, I was so busy thinking that I had missed what Mr Hammond had been saying.

Fortunately, he repeated himself – again and again and again . . .

He LOVES the sound of his own voice.

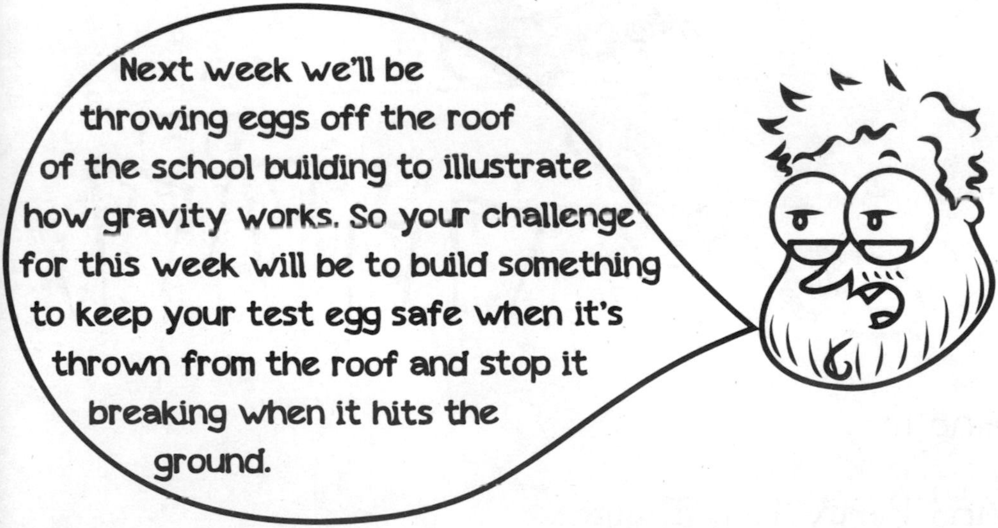
Next week we'll be throwing eggs off the roof of the school building to illustrate how gravity works. So your challenge for this week will be to build something to keep your test egg safe when it's thrown from the roof and stop it breaking when it hits the ground.

This sent my imagination **SOARING!**

I was already imagining Superdog piloting the egg to safety, with everyone standing and looking in awe at him.

And me.

And Percy too, I guess.

The egg will definitely need some kind of parachute

. . . or maybe springs!

(I like springs . . .)

After school Percy and I headed straight for the ~~lab~~ CLUBHOUSE where we began THE INVENTING PROCESS!

First, we looked in all of our shoeboxes and jam jars for inspiration and pulled out a few things that we thought might be useful:

WHAT WE FOUND

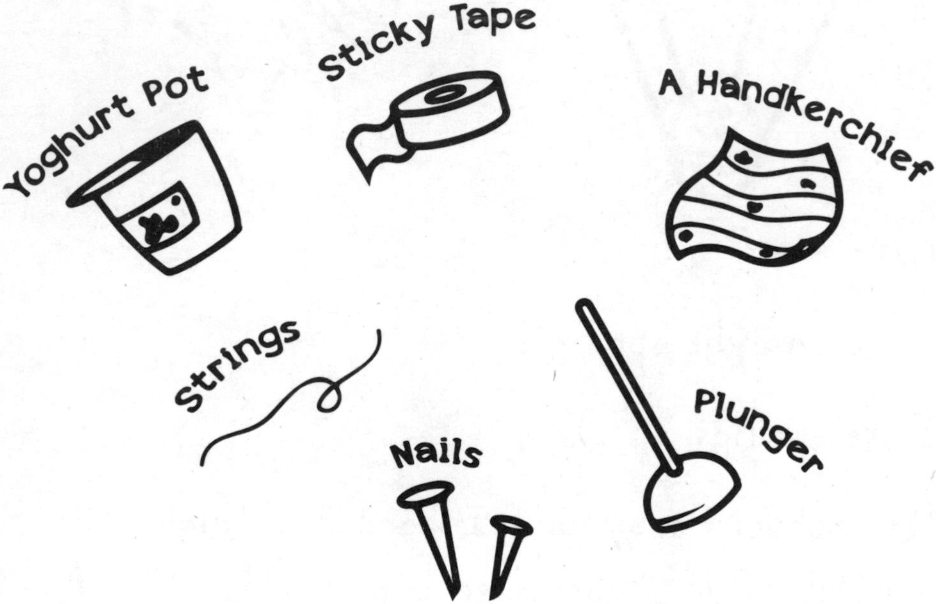

Yoghurt Pot
Sticky Tape
A Handkerchief
Strings
Nails
Plunger

Dad brought us some more baked bean jelly and asked us what we're doing.

We explained that we're looking for things to build an egg protection system with.

Dad looked thoughtful (puts his hand under his chin and squints, like so . . .)

Boys, I think you're going about this all the wrong way. I mean, have you studied the exact nature of an egg? Do you know how an egg breaks?

yes !!

He then said:

BUT DO YOU?
DO YOU REALLY?

Dad seemed REALLY determined to make us admit that we didn't know the first thing about breaking eggs.

So we decided to admit that we didn't know the first thing about breaking eggs.

Dad then went into the house and came back with a dozen eggs.

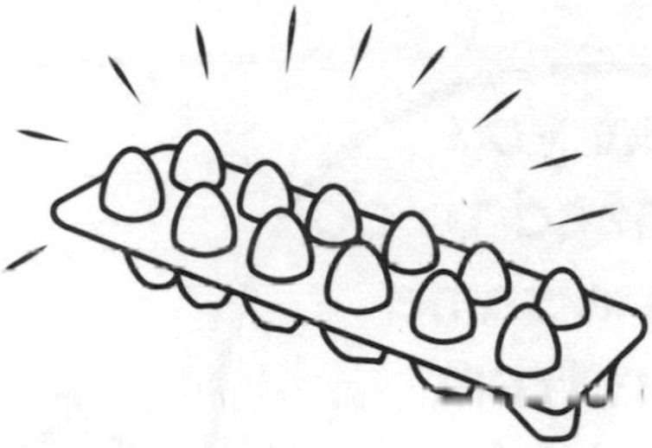

He said that the first thing we had to study was the way an egg dropped from a normal height.

He demonstrated this by dropping an egg on the floor.

It broke.

Percy and I agreed that this was indeed very interesting.

Dad then said:

What you REALLY need to do is study the same phenomenon from different heights, velocities and trajectories

We left the ~~lab~~ (CLUBHOUSE) and ventured out into the garden.

I climbed a tree and asked Dad to pass me an egg.

Dad passed me an egg, and I dropped it.

It broke.

We all found this very interesting.

HOW INTERESTING!!

At this point I told Superdog to start take notes on our experiment.

Percy then cleverly suggested that we should also study sideways trajectory.

He chucked an egg across the garden.

It hit Mum's car, which was parked in the driveway.

This was also very interesting.

And fun!

Dad said:

LOOK AT THE WAY THE EGG SLIDES
OWN THE SIDE OF THE CAR.
THE SMOOTH SURFACE OFFERS
VERY LITTLE RESISTANCE

This, we all felt, was very interesting.

And very important to science.

And to eggs.

So the rest of the experiment was carried out on Mum's car because its surfaces were JUST SO INTERESTING.

I was disappointed when we ran out of eggs, but at least we had learnt that eggs definitely DO break when they hit a solid surface at speed.

Experiment =

A COMPLETE SUCCESS!

Percy and I went over to check Superdog's notes.

He hadn't written anything down.

He **HAD** ripped a grasshopper to bits.

I was very interested by this.

Percy puked (as usual).

All in all, a great day!

I didn't make any really fantastic finds on my way to school this morning:

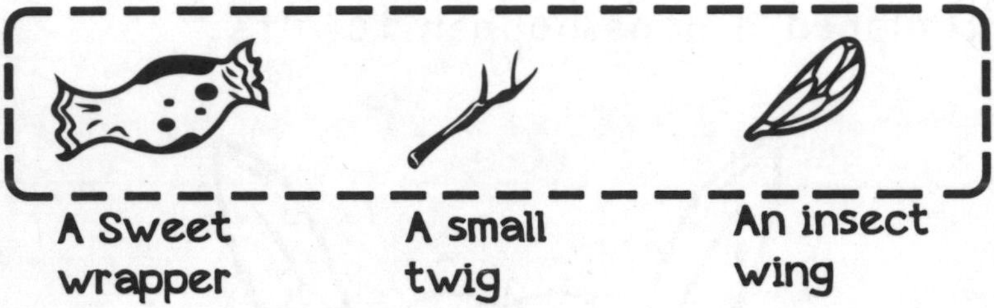
A Sweet wrapper
A small twig
An insect wing

So I decided to spend the morning doodling in my super-secret spy notebook and relaxing.

You see, we had PE later that day and I OBVIOUSLY didn't want to wear myself out or anything.

PE isn't really my thing.

I'm more of a brains person.

Well, except in Maths (BLEURGH!).

I always seem to pass PE though, despite never **ACTUALLY** doing anything.

I think this is because Ms Mills knows that I'm in the Science Club and uses me to get information about Mr Hammond.

Ms Mills used to always ask me things like:

What was Mr. Hammond wearing yesterday?
Do you know where he lives? Do you think he likes Miss Quimby?
Do you think there is a Mrs. Hammond?

And I'd say:

I . . . CAN'T . . . RUN . . . . . . AND . . . TALK . . . AT . . . THE . . . SAME . . . TIME!

So now Ms Mills lets me sit out as long as I tell her EVERYTHING about Mr Hammond.

It's hard to fill an entire hour sharing information about someone I don't really know all that well.

It's hard to do ANYTHING for an entire hour.

But for the sake of getting out of PE I am willing to do ANYTHING.

When I run out of things to say about Mr Hammond, I usually find that making a few details up here and there helps.

This requires me to be inventive.

(Good thing that I am a GENIUS INVENTOR!)

This is why Ms Mills now thinks that Mr Hammond:

- USED TO BE A ROCKET SCIENTIST WORKING FOR NASA

- SPENDS HIS WEEKENDS WRESTLING HAGGIS IN SCOTLAND

- WAS RAISED BY A PACK OF WOLVES IN THE FOREST

- HAS SEEN A YETI TWICE

It's a good thing that Mr Hammond hides whenever he sees Ms Mills.

If they ever got around to talking, I'd be BUSTED!

I'd have to exercise during PE class just like everyone else . . .

NOOOOOOOOO!

Everyone in class was talking about the new METAL FACE movie.

We were all in agreement: it is going to be sheer COOLNESS!

Posters had been put up EVERYWHERE:

- ON WALLS

- ON BILLBOARDS

Metal
Face

- ON . . . well, mostly just on walls and billboards

EVERYONE in class was going.

Debra Derby asked if I was going to go:

Me: I wouldn't miss it! I'm going to go and work for **METAL FACE** one day and invent all his cool things for him - **AND** I'll have a cool nickname too, like Experimental . . . erm . . . Face.

She thought this was **VERY FUNNY** and said:

Debra: Hahaha! "Experimental Face", huh? That's a great nickname for you . . .

I don't think that she really thought that it was a good nickname at all.

Then the bell rang for PE.

So I was in PE, which was bad enough, but . . .

SHOCK HORROR

Today's lesson: Volleyball.

ARGH!

Do you know how much my legs hurt when I play volleyball?

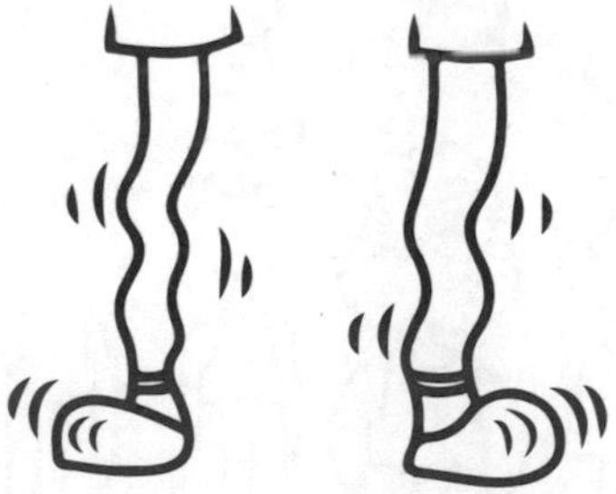

This was definitely a good lesson to try and skip.

I went and stood by Ms Mills.

MR. HAMMOND HAS SET US A NEW SCIENCE PROJECT. WOULD YOU LIKE TO HEAR ABOUT IT?

Ms Mills organised everyone into two teams and said that I can be her helper.

RESULT!

I told Ms Mills all about the new challenge.

THAT ISN'T A NEW CHALLENGE,
YOU KNOW – SCIENCE TEACHERS HAVE BEEN DOING
THAT EXPERIMENT FOR YEARS.
I'M SURE THAT THE BEST WAY OF PROTECTING AN EGG
HAS ALREADY BEEN INVENTED.

I then told Ms Mills how IMPORTANT it was that I got a REALLY GOOD grade in the experiment.

I mean, just imagine if I didn't get to go and see the new Metal Face movie . . .

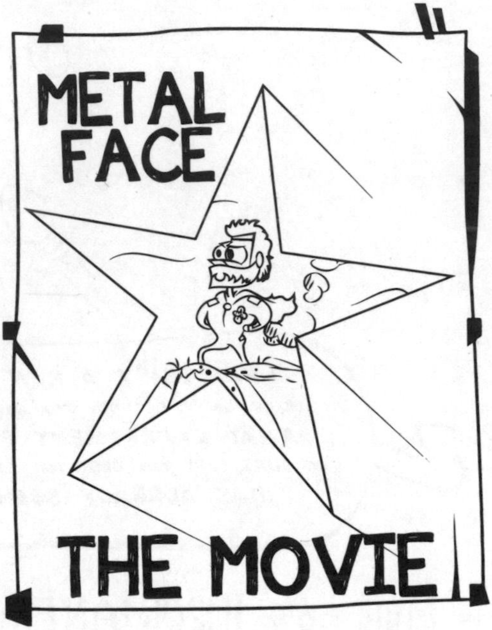
METAL FACE
THE MOVIE

I'd be an outcast . . .

No one would talk to me . . .

And the other kids would NEVER EVER call me Experimental Face, my SUPER-COOL superhero name (and it IS super-cool!).

Ms Mills chuckled and said:

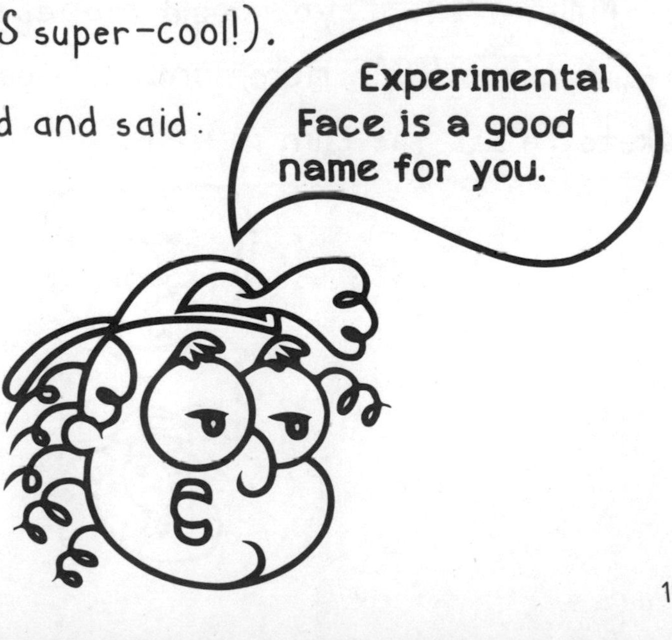
Experimental Face is a good name for you.

I really don't see what everyone finds so funny.

Experimental Face is an excellent name for a

SUPER-INVENTOR.

(And I AM a super-inventor!)

Therefore, I AM EXPERIMENTAL FACE!

Anyway,

Ms Mills then said:

Ms. Mills: Well, if you could manage to set me up on a date with Mr Hammond, I would buy you two tickets to see the film myself.

METAL
FACE

I said that I would try my best.

At least then I would have a backup plan.

Sort of.

Getting Mr Hammond to go on a date with Ms Mills would be much more difficult than getting an A in Science.

It would probably be more difficult than getting an A in Maths!

Okay, maybe not in Maths (BLEURGH!).

When I got home Mum says:

Mum: Have you seen my video camera anywhere? Mel is about to take her first steps and I don't want to miss it.

Uh oh!

I look behind her.

Mel is walking happily from one end of the living room to the other.

She's strolling.

She's practically jogging!

I don't like to disappoint her though, so I told Mum that I hadn't seen the camera and suggested that she looks somewhere else . . . outdoors maybe, or in the car.

Oh!

ARGH!

But definitely DO NOT look in the living room or in the outdoor dustbin!

It won't be there!

Definitely not!

No chance!

I decided that it was a good time to go and hide in my room and get started on my science project.

(I had not actually STARTED my science project . . .)

(I should probably have started my science project . . .)

GENIUS
AT
WORK
KEEP OUT

I thought long and hard about clever ways to protect my egg, but all that kept going through my mind was Ms Mills saying that "the best way of protecting the egg has ALREADY BEEN INVENTED . . ."

That, and: "**Experimental Face** is a good nickname for you."

Which is true – it is!

Suddenly I had a super-inventive idea - a cracking idea that will stop my egg from cracking!

(Hahaha!) 

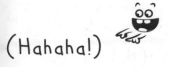

I rushed downstairs and out of the house (stopping to borrow some money from Mum) and ~~sprinted~~ ~~ran~~ ~~jogged~~ walked very fast down the street towards the nearest convenience store.

I knew EGGSactly what I had to do.

(Hahaha!) 

We had all gathered after school for Science Club.

I was feeling pretty confident.

I'd nailed this.

Mr Hammond took us all up onto the roof of the school building.

Smug, full-of-himself, twit-faced Gareth Trumpshaw insisted that he got to go first.

Gareth Trumpshaw is such a twit.

TWIT

Gareth opened a box and took out an impressive-looking piece of equipment covered in wires and flashing lights.

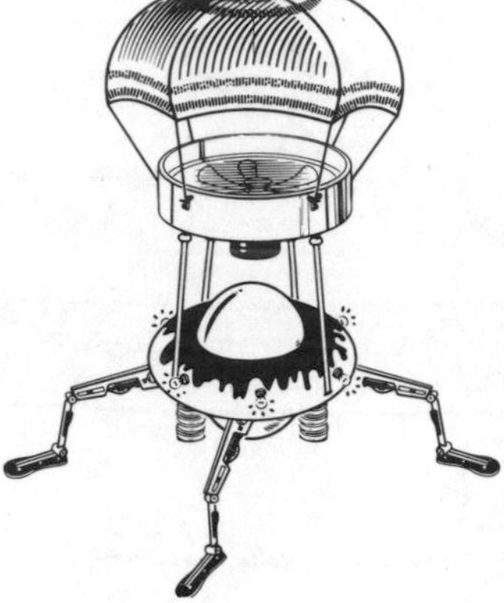

Things weren't looking good.

Smug, full-of-himself, twit-faced Gareth Trumpshaw's contraption:

- A doughnut-shaped ring, which holds the egg
- A series of legs and springs underneath, to cushion the landing of the contraption
- A fan and a parachute, to help the contraption to float to the ground

Gareth took out a remote control.

The contraption walked to the edge of the building.

The contraption gently leapt off.

The contraption's fans started whirring, forcing air up into the parachute.

The contraption's parachute inflated.

The contraption landed gently on the ground.

Stupid Gareth.

Percy went next.

He had wrapped his egg in a ton of bubble wrap squished tightly into a ball.

This was less impressive.

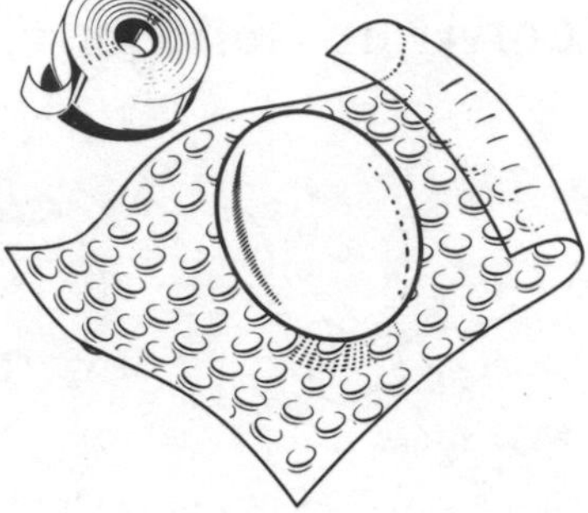

Debra Derby had covered two tea strainers in springs and glued them both together.

Nitty Neil (who has nits) had filled an envelope with cotton wool.

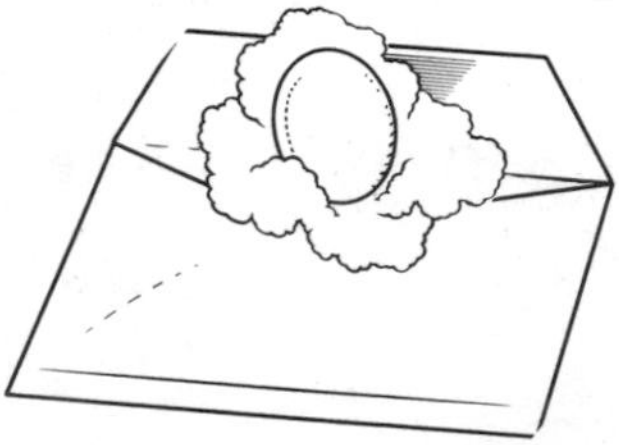

THAT was his big idea?

An envelope?

Honestly!

His idea looked even more last-minute than mine!

Next up was Belinda, then Leo, then Michael . . .

Actually, I was seeing quite a lot of envelopes and cotton wool.

Sorry, Neil . . .

Finally it was my turn.

I reached into my bag and pulled out . . .

THE MIGHTY EGG CARTON

Everyone looked REALLY unimpressed.

I threw it off the roof and it hit the ground with a thud.

Everyone still looked really unimpressed.

Mr Hammond took us all downstairs to see whose eggs had survived.

Smug, full-of-himself, twit-faced Gareth's smug, full-of-itself, twit-shelled egg was in perfect condition.

Twit.

Percy unwrapped his egg. . .

...he unwrapped...

...and unwrapped...

...and unwrapped.

(How much bubble wrap did you use, Percy?)

It was broken.

Mr Hammond inspected the egg and said that it would probably have survived but Percy had wrapped it too tightly.

He said that he had probably broken it whilst wrapping it at home.

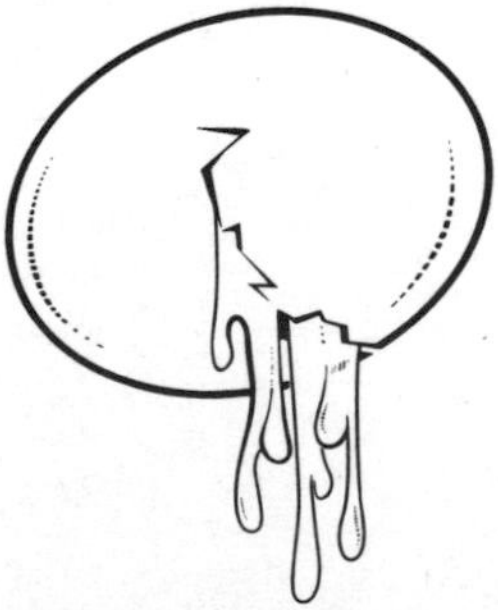

Why, Percy, WHY?

Debra Derby's egg almost survived, but Mr Hammond noticed a crack in it.

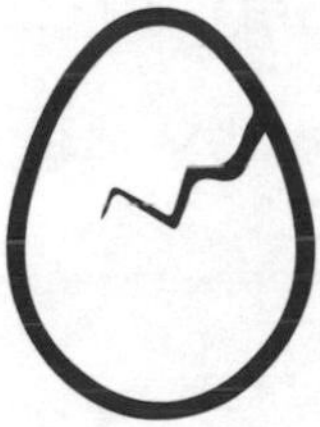

Poor Debra.

Poor Debra's egg.

Nitty Neil (who has nits) looked confident, but Nitty Neil's egg (which didn't have nits) was broken.

Belinda's egg: broken

Leo's egg: broken

Michael's egg: broken

Mr Hammond then went to inspect my egg.

He tried to open **THE MIGHTY EGG CARTON**, but it wasn't as easy as it looked.

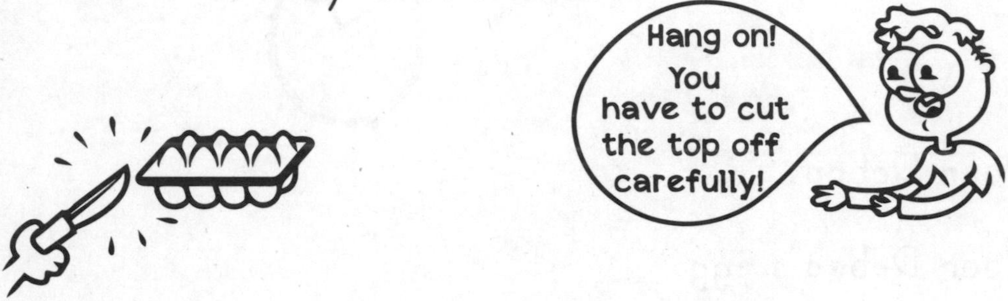
Hang on! You have to cut the top off carefully!

Mr Hammond cut away the top of **THE MIGHTY EGG CARTON** and inside, for the entire world (everyone in Science Club) to see, was my PERFECTLY UNDAMAGED EGG, suspended in . . .

You guessed it!

JELLY!

Mr Hammond: Oh, very clever Danny, very clever – well done! And I think that you deserve some extra credit for using such common everyday items . . ."

Yes, I thought I did too.

I felt SMUG.

I'd got a whopping great A+!

A+

AND I got lots of praise from Mum and Dad!

AND I knew that I would get to see the Metal Face Movie!

AND I won't have to convince Mr Hammond to go out with Ms Mills!

RESULT!

At the end of Science Club, Mr Hammond told us all about the upcoming end-of-term challenge.

Mr Hammond: The end-of-term challenge will be to build your own soap box racer. You can do this in teams of two.

SOAP BOX RACE

Smug, full-of-himself, twit-faced Gareth complained that he wanted to work on his own.

Mr Hammond said okay, but only because there are an uneven number of students in Science Club (and because no one likes working with Gareth).

Gareth always prefers to enter challenges on his own because he thinks he's smarter than everybody else.

He isn't.

He's a twit.

Mr Hammond then handed us all an instruction sheet so that we knew what we could and couldn't use.

INSTRUCTIONS

What we needed:

- Wheels
- Wood
- Some rope to steer
- A pivot so that we can turn the front wheels
- A soap box or other container to sit in

Optional items:

- Breaks
- An improved steering system
- Decoration
- A homemade propulsion system

Forbidden items:

- Prefabricated kits
- Go-karts
- Ready-made engines (motorcycle, lawnmower, etc.)
- Actual mechanical car parts

Mr Hammond then told us that there will be a race to determine the winner.

It was to be called the **SCIENCE CLUB SOAP BOX DERBY** and the winner would get to go to . . .

METALWAY,
THE METAL FACE THEME PARK!

1st
METALWAY

I was so confident after my PHENOMENAL success in the egg challenge that I just KNEW that those tickets are as good as mine!

I couldn't wait to start work on . . .

The unstoppable...

METAL-MOBILE!

(After telling Mum and Dad about my fantastic A+, of course!)

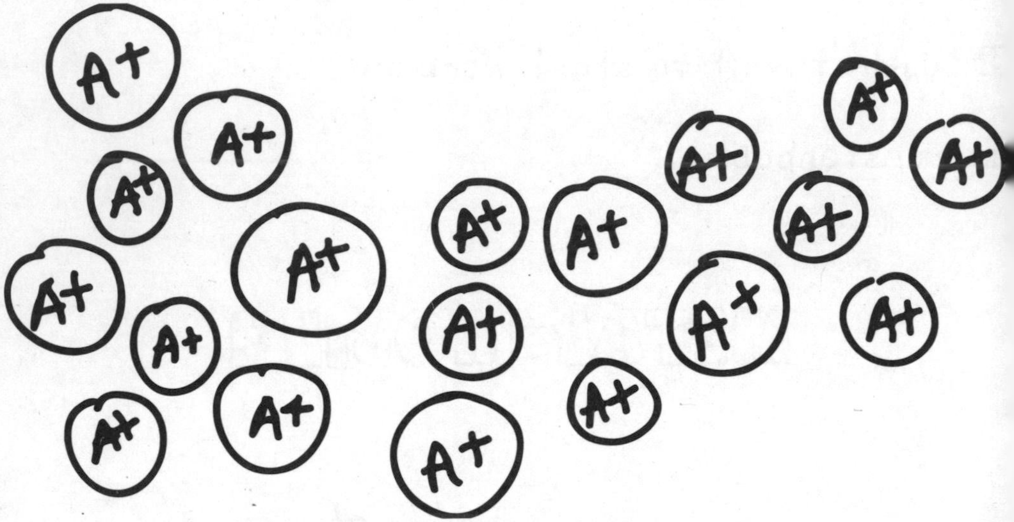
A+
A+
A+
A+
A+
A+
A+
A+
A+
A+
A+
A+
A+
A+
A+
A+
A+
A+
A+

What a COOL day!

Everything worked out really well, and no one even noticed that I had boiled my egg before putting it in the jelly!

You know, just in case . . .

I've been really busy over the past few days and haven't had time to make many notes in my super-secret spy notebook.

This is because Percy and I have been working very hard on the design for the almighty. . .

METAL-MOBILE!

Dad has been really helpful and has given us LOTS of ideas.

According to Dad, the soap box racer will need:

- Wheels
- A base
- A steering system
- A propulsion system
- Some SUPER-COOL decorations

SOAP

Percy and I have been spending most of our time working on the super-cool decorations, as we felt that this was DEFINITELY the most important part of any successful soap box racer.

As it was the METAL Mobile, we thought that it should look, well, metal-y.

However, we couldn't find much metal just lying about.

So we decided to cover it in tin foil instead.

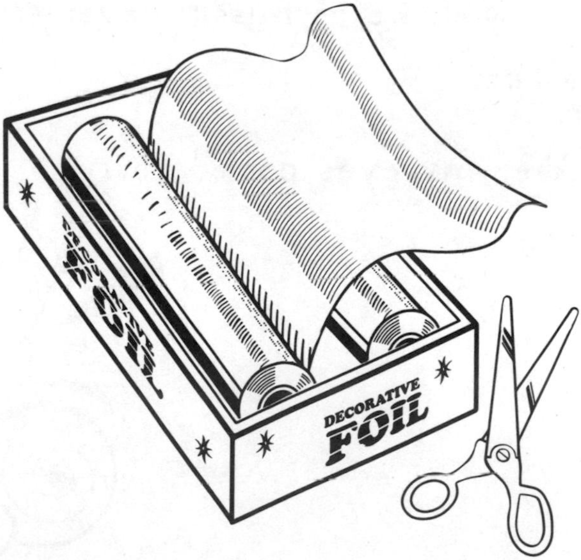
DECORATIVE FOIL

We found an old cardboard fridge box and fashioned some **SUPER-COOL FINS** to go on the back of the racer.

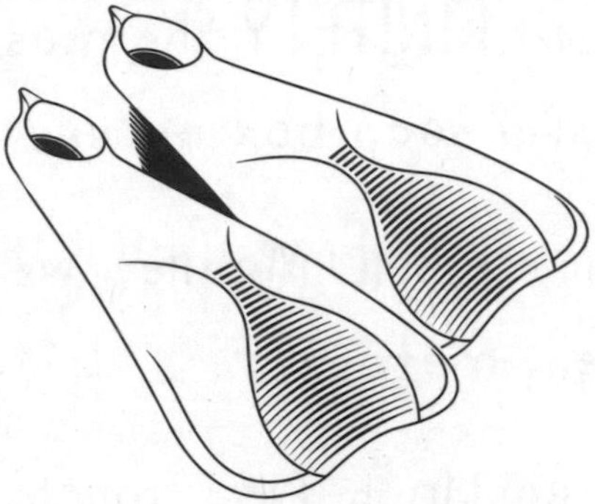

Percy and I have worked hard on the fins, but we're still missing:

- Erm . . . well, we're missing everything except for the fins.

I'd better keep my eyes peeled then.

We've FINALLY been to go to see the Metal Face movie!

It seemed like I'd been waiting FOREVER!

Dad and I got in the car and went to pick up Percy.

I decided to take Superdog with me, as it is what Metal Face would have wanted.

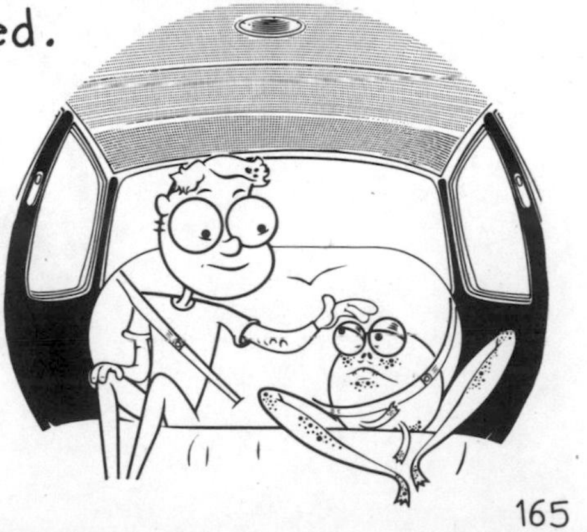

When Percy got in the car Dad lets us in on a little surprise:

He had brought us some EXTRA-SPECIAL SPROUT JELLY!

He said that he has already tested it.

Then he farted.

The fart was SO POTENT that we were all nearly SICK!

Needless to say, we were all REALLY IMPRESSED with the results, so Percy and I wolfed down the rest of the sprout jelly in hope that it would take effect before we got to the movies.

Dad spent the whole journey talking about the Metal-Mobile. He was REALLY excited about it - even more than Percy and me.

In fact, quite a lot more than Percy and me . . .

He kept saying things like:

The best wheels are those old pram wheels.
We have to think of an ingenious propulsion

- "You'd be amazed at the treasures you can find if you just go through people's dustbins . . ."

Percy and I thought that "propulsion system" sounded funny, and every time Dad said it one of us farted.

Blah, blah, blah propulsion system...
"...Paaaarrffffff"

METAL FACE

There was a REALLY long queue to buy tickets.

I recognised a lot of kids from school.

There was a lot of excitement, a lot of farting, and a lot of parents saying things like: "Knock it off or we're going home!"

We were all very excited until suddenly . . .

HORROR OF HORRORS!

Who should queue up behind us but smug, full-of-himself, twit-faced Gareth Trumpshaw and his dad!

Gareth and I both looked away as if we hadn't seen each other, but Gareth's dad spurted out:

JAMES ? JAMES DINGLE?
HOW ON EARTH ARE YOU DOING!
I HAVE'T SEEN YOU SINCE...
SINCE YOU FIRED ME.

Everybody looked uncomfortable.

Gareth's dad didn't want to make a scene and said:

YES- UNFORTUNATE BUSINESS, THAT...
I WAS HOPING WE COULD PUT IT BEHIND US.

To which Dad replied:

yes- it was YOU who put me to work on improving the firework dispensing machine! YOU were to blame as well! But YOU put all the blame on ME

To which Gareth's dad said:

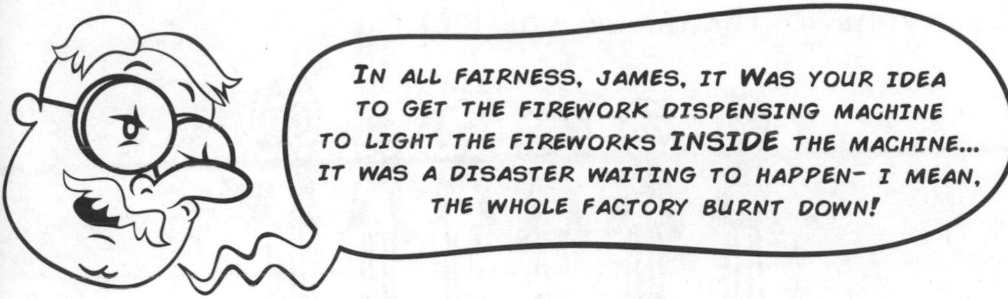
IN ALL FAIRNESS, JAMES, IT WAS YOUR IDEA TO GET THE FIREWORK DISPENSING MACHINE TO LIGHT THE FIREWORKS INSIDE THE MACHINE... IT WAS A DISASTER WAITING TO HAPPEN- I MEAN, THE WHOLE FACTORY BURNT DOWN!

Then there was a deadly silence.

Everyone in the queue was looking.

Nobody moved.

A tumbleweed rolled past.

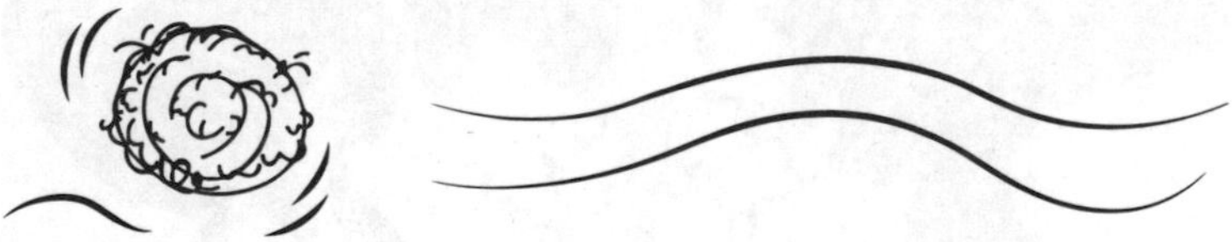

Then the jelly finally took effect, and Percy farted.

The Metal Face movie was UNBELIEVABLE!

The movie theatre had one of those SUPER-LOUD SOUND SYSTEMS!

Every time Metal Face belched or farted, the whole cinema shook!

There was even one bit where Pudding Breath drowns a small village in an ocean of CURDLED CUSTARD PUKE!

It felt so real . . . it was like I was actually there being showered in vomit!

Then I realised that the sprout jelly hadn't agreed with Percy and he'd thrown up (as usual).

But that's okay - nothing, not even Percy's sick, could spoil the AWESOMENESS of that movie!

Superdog sat through the whole movie in awe, without saying a word.

Dad was acting weirdly all the way back home.

He kept muttering to himself, saying things like:

- "I'll show you fireworks dispensers . . ."
- "Disaster waiting to happen, huh . . . "
- "We'll see who has the last laugh . . ."

I'm no expert (even though I AM a genius) but I'd say that he was angry with Mr Trumpshaw.

OR he was suffering from sprout gas poisoning.

Or both!

I haven't scribbled much recently as Percy, Dad, Superdog and I have been preparing for the soap box derby.

SCIENCE
CLUB SOAP BOX
Saturday 21st
To be held
in Swan Lake
Park
1st
price
4 tickets to
Metalway
Amusement
Park

Dad has been taking the derby very seriously.

This is both good AND bad.

Why this is BAD:

- He has taken control of the entire project! We think that this is because he sees it as his way of getting revenge on smug, full-of-himself, twit-faced Gareth's dad. Percy and I don't get to have much of a say anymore, so we mostly sat around making SUPER-COOL METAL FACE COSTUMES using tin foil.

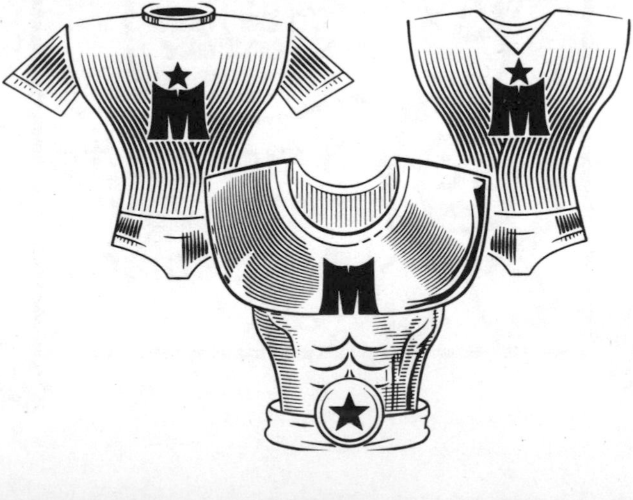

M
M
M

Why this is **GOOD**:

- He has taken control of the entire project! This means that Percy and I don't have to do very much and now have more time to make SUPER-COOL METAL FACE COSTUMES using tin foil.

Dad has helped us to find all of the parts that we were missing, such as:

- **WHEELS**

Dad said that the best kinds of wheels are the ones you get on those big old-fashioned prams.

I told Dad that you don't see many old-fashioned prams anymore.

That is, except for Mel's pram.

Which **WAS** also mine . . .

THE SHAME!

Dad didn't want to upset Mum by taking the wheels off of Mel's pram and her finding out (that it was him).

So he waited until she'd taken Mel for a stroll down to the shop.

Mum left the pram outside and took Mel into the shops to buy some milk and a magazine and to have one of those LOOOOOONG natters with Mrs Elton, the shopkeeper.

OPEN

Dad secretly followed her and hid in the bushes (secretly).

As soon as Mum had gone inside, Dad (very secretly) got to work getting the wheels off.

When Mum returned, she found that there were no wheels on the pram.

She was quite upset about this.

But she wasn't upset at US.

THAT'S the most important thing.

- **PIVOT**

Dad said that we'd need a really good-quality bolt to use as a pivot in the steering mechanism.

These aren't very expensive to buy.

However, Dad just so HAPPENED to notice a little decorative windmill in Mrs Bergenstein's garden, and the bolt that attached the sails to the windmill just so HAPPENED to be the perfect size for our pivot.

Dad decided that it couldn't hurt to borrow it for a bit.

It **WOULD** be silly not to . . .

So he waited until it was dark, then he crept secretly into Mrs Bergenstein's garden and secretly borrowed the bolt.

He didn't want to upset her though, so he replaced it with a super-secret rusty nail from my super-secret stash.

Secretly.

This clever solution worked REALLY well . . . at first.

Unfortunately, there was a big gust of wind that night and the sails came loose and whizzed off at high speed, chopping the head off of one of Mrs Bergenstein's prized garden gnomes.

It was an REALLY ugly gnome though, so in a way we were doing her a favour . . .

- BASE

Dad realised that we'd also need some good strong pieces of wood to build the base with.

He'd noticed that Mr Patel (from down the road) had recently replaced his garden fence.

Once again, under the cover of night, Dad went around to Mr Patel's house and borrowed a few boards from the fence in his back garden.

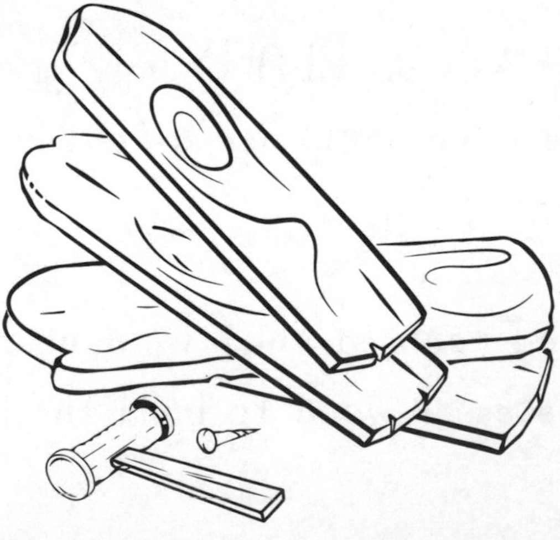

Unfortunately, what Dad DIDN'T know about Mr Patel was that he is an ostrich farmer and had recently bought four ostriches to go on his farm.

This came as quite a surprise to us all on the next morning when we discovered that every garden on the street had been trashed and covered in poo.

We couldn't be sure that the ostriches were the culprits, but they were looking MIGHTY SUSPICIOUS (and not to mention RELIEVED) . . .

We also found out that ostriches can be quite violent when they think that they're being accused of something.

Mr Patel got pecked on the nose as he tried to round them up.

Pest control **AND** the riot police had to be called in.

It was HILARIOUS!

- SOAP BOX

We weren't able to find a soap box (because soap doesn't come in big wooden boxes anymore).

However, as luck would have it, the back seats in Mum's car slid right out.

It's like they **WANTED** to be borrowed!

Dad had to drill quite a lot of holes in them so that the racer would be safe (I'm sure Mum won't mind), and Percy and I **HAD** to paint them so that they matched the rest of the racer (this, Mum **MIGHT** mind).

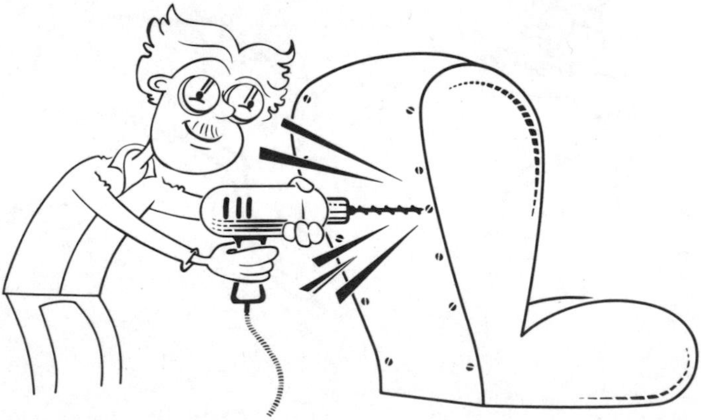

But the MOST IMPORTANT thing of all is the . . .

- **PROPULSION SYSTEM**

Dad was working on this for weeks, and the result was sheer GENIUS!

On either side of the racer Dad had attached a super-fantastic, super-amazing and (best of all) super-fizzy bottle of SPROUT COLA!

SC

Each bottle had been mounted on springs (I like springs).

All we had to do is shake the bottles REALLY, REALLY HARD so that the pressure built up.

Then we just had to release the nozzles, giving us an almighty BOOOOOOST!

BOOOOST

So here we are.

After a lot of work and a lot (and I mean A LOT) of upset neighbors, behold the wonder that is . . .

THE METAL-MOBILE!

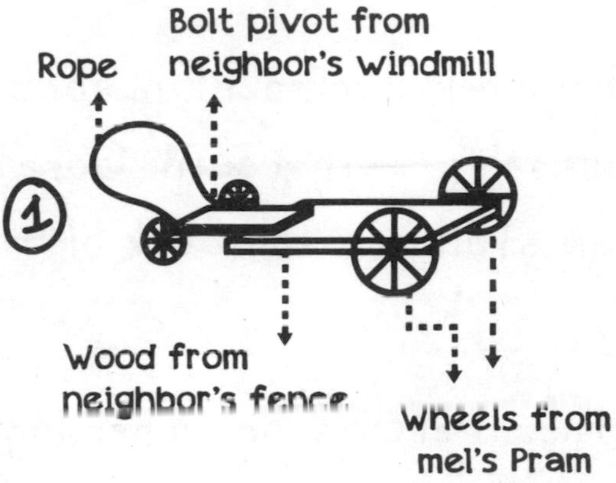

Bolt pivot from neighbor's windmill
Rope
1
Wood from neighbor's fence
Wheels from mel's Pram

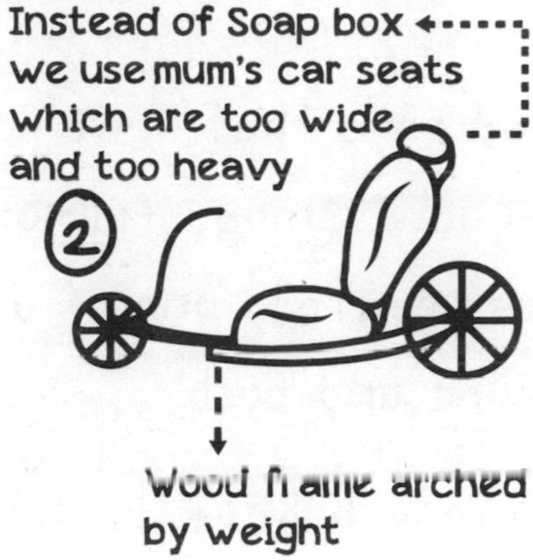

Instead of Soap box we use mum's car seats which are too wide and too heavy
2
Wood frame arched by weight

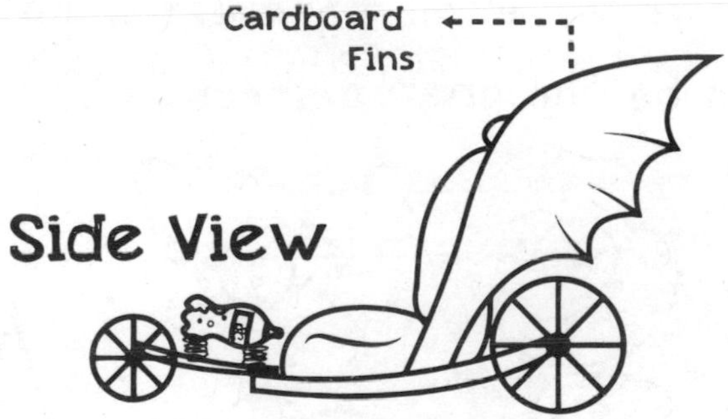

Cardboard Fins
Side View

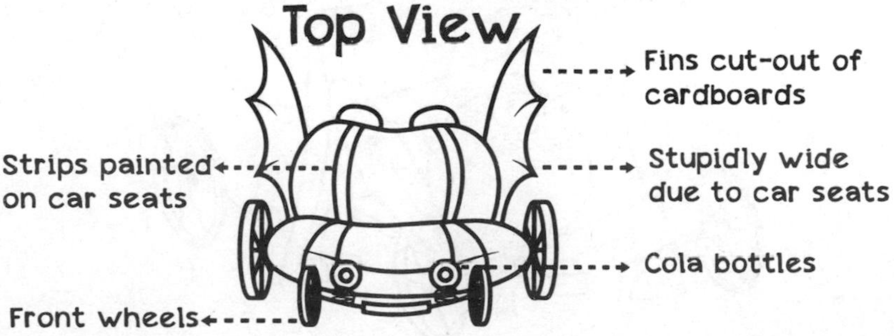

Top View
Fins cut-out of cardboards
Strips painted on car seats
Stupidly wide due to car seats
Cola bottles
Front wheels

Not bad, eh?

Dad says that if we fall behind in the race (probably because smug, full-of-himself, twit-faced Gareth has cheated) one of us can stand on the back of the racer and push.

That will have to be either Percy's or Superdog's job, because we have all agreed (I have decided) that I should be the one to steer.

The **BIG DAY** finally arrives.

The Science Club Soap Box Derby is being held in Swan Lake Park, which is just behind the school.

WELOME TO SWANLAKE

Mr Hammond said that it needed to be held somewhere with a steep hill.

Swan Lake Park has a VERY steep hill.

A VERY steep hill that runs down next to a DUCK POND!

HERO

GULP.

Some of the parents have said things like:

It's an outrage!
What a dangerous idea!
They're all going to die!

They don't want their kids to enter the race.

This is BRILLIANT NEWS!

The fewer racers there are in the race, the better our chances are of winning those four tickets to METALWAY!

METAL WAY

Percy and I had been putting a lot of work into the Metal Mobile, so we'd fallen behind on ~~some most~~ all of our other homework assignments.

REPORT CARD
D
F
F
D

Dad doesn't seem to mind though.

All he can think about is REVENGE!

He says that smug, full-of-himself, twit-faced Gareth is bound to get his smug, full-of-himself, twit-faced dad to build his racer for him using lots of "cutting-edge technology" from AcmeTech.

He says that he's going to be "watching them like a hawk."

We were going to put the racer in the back of Mum's car and drive it to the park, but bits of it are too wide to fit in the car (bits of it are the car) so we've had to tow it.

So we got to the park - there wasn't much of a crowd:

- Mr Norton, looking miserable

- Miss Quimby, looking hungry

- Ms Mills, looking scary

- Mr Hammond, looking invisible (he was hiding from Ms Mills)

Mr. Hammond

Percy and I decided to check out the other teams.

Not many people had entered.

RESULT!

Debra Derby and Amy Almond had decorated their racer like a giant roller skate and called themselves The Skid Marks.

THE SKID MARKS

Yeah, we all laughed too.

Nitty Neil (who has nits) and Belinda (who does not - or at least did not, but might now) had been convinced by Belinda's mum to dress up like historical characters and turn their soap box racer into a cart from some old period in history.

'?'

They hadn't thought of a name.

Neil looked really fed-up and embarrassed.

I would have been too - he looked ridiculous!

Leo and Michael had painted flames down the sides of their racer and called themselves the Evil Suds.

Evil Suds

And then there was smug, full-of-himself, twit-faced Gareth.

His racer looked impressive.

It was covered in flashing lights, painted yellow and called the Custard Cruiser.

Smug, full-of-himself, twit-faced Gareth and his Dad had matching yellow t-shirts with "Go Team Custard!" printed on them.

GO
TEAM
CUSTARD
GO
TEAM
CUSTARD
CUSTARD CRUISER

Twits.

Gareth's dad waved politely at my dad and my dad waved (shook his fist) politely (angrily) back.

Then he did that hand gesture signal thing that means "I'm watching you".

We were all terribly embarrassed by that hand gesture signal thing.

We all hoped that he wouldn't do it again.

Mr Hammond then called the teams up to the top of the hill and explained the rules:

AS YOU CAN ALL SEE, THERE'S ABOUT HALF A MILE BETWEEN THIS POINT HERE AND THAT POINT DOWN THERE.

He pointed to the finish line, which he's painted on the ground to the right hand side of the duck pond at the bottom of the hill.

NOW THEN, YOU LOT - JUST LINE YOUR RACERS UP HERE AND WE'LL ALL GO TO WAIT FOR YOU AT THE FINISH LINE.
WHEN I BLOW MY WHISTLE, THE RACE BEGINS. THE WINNER WILL BE THE FIRST RACER TO CROSS THE FINISH LINE
(WITHOUT TAKING THE OBVIOUS SHORT CUT THROUGH THE DUCK POND)

(Ducks looking scared)

Excuse me Mr. Hammond, but this is a very steep hill - won't all the children end up in the duck
My dear, this is a SCIENCE CLUB CHALLENGE. I'm sure that everyone has been sensible enough to have developed sturdy steering systems and reliable breaks for their racers, rather than just making them go fast and look fancy.

Everybody looked around.

Steering . . . system . . . ?

Breaks . . . ?

It was clear that most of us had spent more time worrying about decorating our racers or finding ways to make them go faster than worrying about how to control them, let alone stop them.

D'oh!

So we were all DOOMED.

But it was too late to back out.

Metalway tickets are at stake here!

All the grown-ups headed for the bottom of the hill (to watch) whilst all the racers took their places at the start line (to PANIC).

Smug, full-of-himself, twit-faced Gareth was right next to us in the Custard Cruiser.

He pulled down his racing goggles, gave me an evil glare and said:

You're TOAST, Dingle

I realise now that I should have said something clever like: "Eat my dust, custard cretin!"

But, at the time, all that I could actually think to say was: "Yeah, well . . . you're MARMALADE!"

Suddenly the whistle blew, and we were off!

I had imagined that we would all shoot off like in the races you see on the telly.

It wasn't like the races you see on the telly.

Smug, full-of-himself, twit-faced Gareth disappeared in a puff of smoke.

Everyone else . . . well, they didn't.

The Skid Marks got off to the next best (or least worst) start, followed by the Period Mobile and the Evil Suds, and they all started to roll gently down the hill.

You might've said that they'd made a CLEAN getaway!

Hahaha!

Y'know, SOAP box racer . . . ?

CLEAN . . . ?

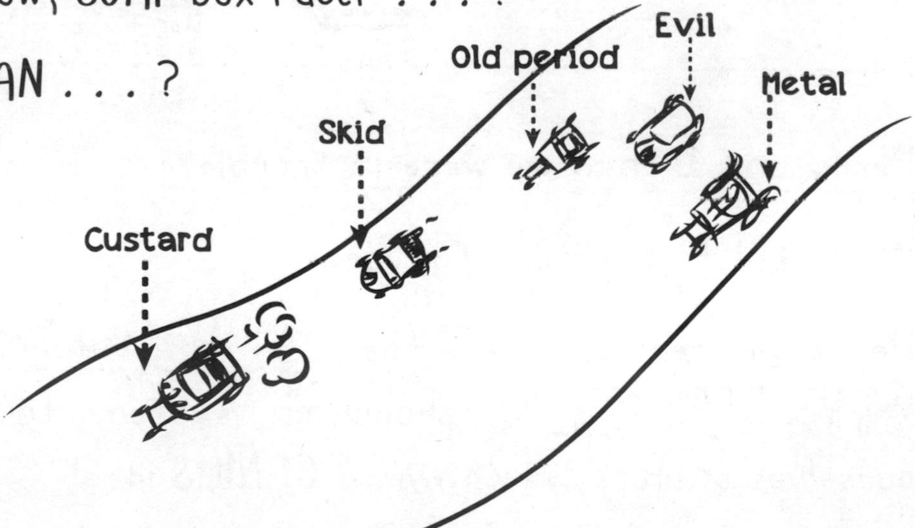
Evil
Old period
Metal
Skid
Custard

Anyway,

The Metal Mobile, meanwhile, didn't want to move.

The weight of the car seats pushed the back wheels down into the mud and was acting like a brake.

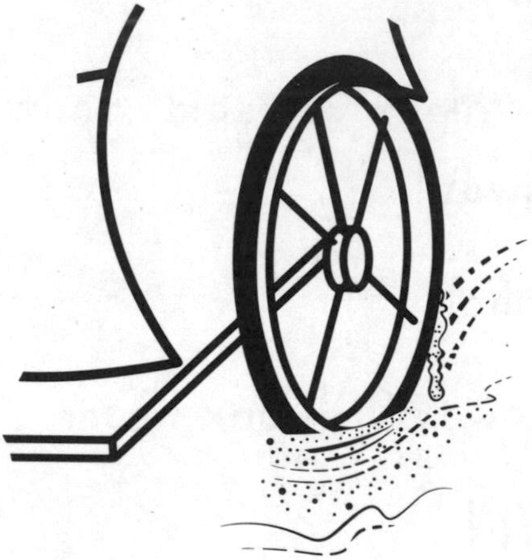

Percy and I knew we were in trouble.

We looked to Superdog for ideas.

He suggested we use the SUPER-FIZZY SPROUT COLA propulsion system to get ourselves unstuck, which was a GENIUS idea!

TECHNICALLY, he just ribbited, but we both understood what he meant (he IS telepathic).

SPROUT

Percy and I each shook a bottle as hard as we could, held onto our seats and released the pressure!

We were expecting an almighty BANG!

SPROUT

What we got was a lot of fizzing as most of the cola drizzled out of the bottles onto the ground.

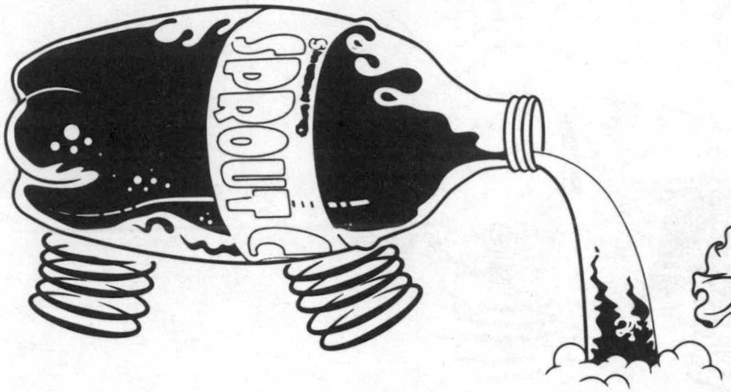
SPROUT

Hmm.

Although it wasn't quite the effect we'd hoped for, the racer was at least a bit lighter.

With Percy and Superdog pushing (I think Superdog is more of a thinker than a pusher) we managed to get the racer moving down the hill.

At this point, smug, full-of-himself, twit-faced Gareth's Custard Cruiser crossed the finish line, and although I couldn't see my Dad's face, I'm sure that he looked GUTTED!

Fortunately (for us) the Evil Suds lost control of their racer at the bottom the hill and crashed into the Skid Marks and the Period Mobile, which propelled them all into the duck pond.

You might've said that they were all WASHED up!

Hahaha! 

Y'know, SOAP box racer . . . ?

WASHED up . . . ?

Anyway,

The Metal Mobile carried on, slowly (VERY slowly) but surely sliding down the hill.

We passed the pile-up in the duck pond and were on our way to a respectable second place when suddenly . . .

The Metal Mobile ground to a halt just short of the finish line!

FINISHING

We were on a flat bit, and the racer was too heavy to roll!

Percy and I looked at each other deep in the eyes.

We knew what we have to do.

We each took a bottle of what remained of the Super-Fizzy Sprout Cola and gulped down the dregs as quickly as possible.

Within seconds it took effect.

With a **SUPER-MASSIVE GAS BUILD-UP** the likes of which has never been known . . .

It took all of our strength . . .

. . . and concentration . . .

. . . but with one huge PAAAAAAAAARF we managed to fart the racer across the finish line!

Hurray for fart-power!!!!!

I'd expected some applause, but the look of sheer horror on everybody's faces was reward enough.

Metal Face would have been proud.

Miss Quimby breaks the silence by saying:

Err...Ahem...There's a small buffet just over there, which you're all welcome to once you've helped get the other racers out of the duck pond...

Percy, Dad, Superdog and I helped ourselves to the buffet whilst we waited for the award ceremony to begin.

All the other kids gradually joined us

They were all soaking wet and smelling of duck wee.

(They could probably have done with some soap, hahaha!)

Mr Hammond eventually appeared and said:

AS YOU ALL KNOW, THE FIRST PRIZE FOR WINNING THE SCIENCE CLUB SOAP BOX DERBY IS FOUR TICKETS TO METALWAY . . .

Everyone looked really disappointed.

That is, everyone except for smug, full-of-himself, twit-faced Gareth.

He looked smug.

And full-of-himself.

And like a twit.

BUT EVERYONE WHO TOOK PART GETS A RUNNERS-UP PRIZE . . . THE NEW METAL FACE ACTION FIGURE, WITH REAL GAS SOUND EFFECTS!

Everybody cheered!

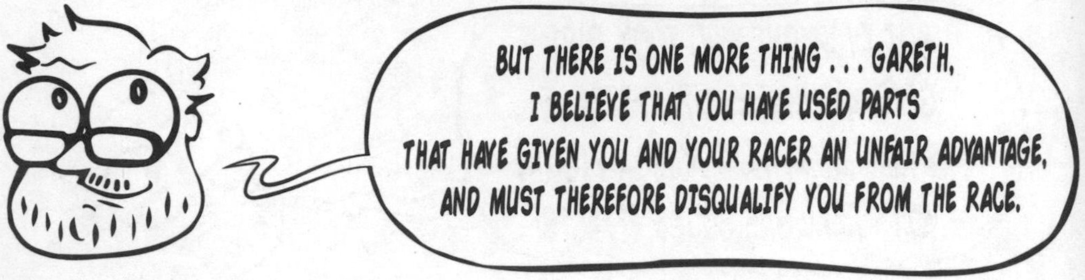
BUT THERE IS ONE MORE THING . . . GARETH, I BELIEVE THAT YOU HAVE USED PARTS THAT HAVE GIVEN YOU AND YOUR RACER AN UNFAIR ADVANTAGE, AND MUST THEREFORE DISQUALIFY YOU FROM THE RACE.

Smug, full-of-himself, twit-faced Gareth didn't look so smug anymore!

In fact, he looked REALLY SHOCKED, and his dad looked REALLY CROSS.

He said:

Parts that give him an unfair advantage? Like what?!

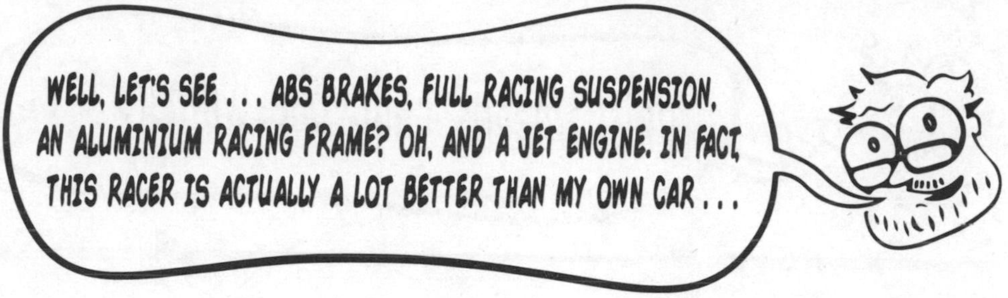
WELL, LET'S SEE . . . ABS BRAKES, FULL RACING SUSPENSION, AN ALUMINIUM RACING FRAME? OH, AND A JET ENGINE. IN FACT, THIS RACER IS ACTUALLY A LOT BETTER THAN MY OWN CAR . . .

Gareth's dad: Oh, that . . .

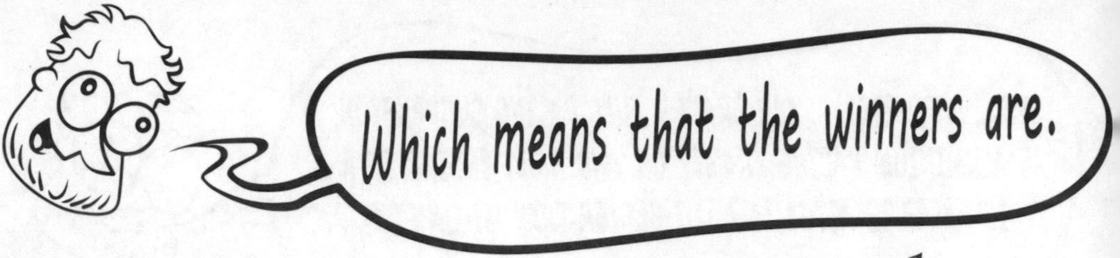
Which means that the winners are.

(Drum roll . . .)

Danny Dingle and Percy McDuff in the Metal Mobile!

RESULT!

RESULT!

RESULT!

1st
1

Needless to say, we are BUBBLING OVER with happiness!

Y'know, bubbles . . . ?

Soap . . . ?

Anyway,

Metalway, here we come!

Look out for book two:

The Super-sonic Submarine

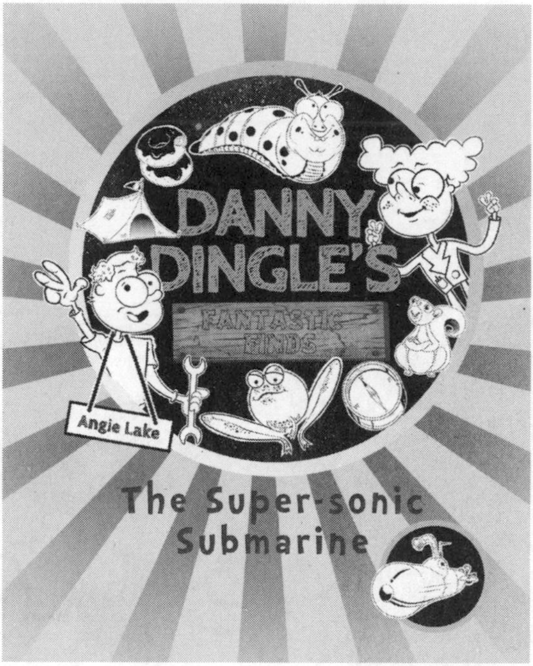
DANNY DINGLE'S
FANTASTIC FINDS
Angie Lake
The Super-sonic Submarine

ISBN: 978-1-78226-260-2

Pre-order your copy today from your favourite bookstore.